MW00940021

The Outlaw's Key

Angeli Perrow

Wishing you adventure!

Angeli Perrow

2017

Mustang Books

Cover format by Michele Bonin
www.michelebonin.com

Copyright @ 2014 Angeli Perrow
Mustang Books
All rights reserved

ISBN-13:978-1505201956
ISBN-10:1505201950

DEDICATION

In memory of my brother Scott, with love

Chapter 1. Noises in the Night

The flickering flames reflected on the faces of the four children sitting around the campfire. Beyond the circle of light, the tall trunks of California redwoods towered above them like dark giants. In the light wind, the trees' branches, hidden high overhead, creaked and groaned like a haunted house.

A sudden high-pitched screech made them all jump.

"What was that?" Christianne asked, her eyes big in the firelight. She huddled closer to her cousin Mandy on the log seat.

"It's Bigfoot coming to get you!" her brother Nick said, raising his arms and growling at her. "Grrrr."

"Cut it out, Nick," Mandy scolded. To her young cousin she said, "Don't worry, Christianne. We're safe here."

"It's probably just an owl out hunting for its dinner," Noah said. "When Mom and Dad said I could go camping with you, I read all about the animals here in California. We have some of the same animals where I live in Florida – bears, raccoons, cougars, and even condors. We have owls that sound just like that." He stuck a marshmallow on a stick and held it over the fire.

"I hope there aren't any alligators!" said Christianne, lifting her feet onto the bench.

"Don't worry," said Noah. "The only alligators here are in zoos."

"Did you read about Bigfoot?" Nick asked. 'These are his stomping grounds, for sure. I watched this video on YouTube where Bigfoot popped out of the bushes and ran right across a clearing. The person watching got the whole thing on his phone camera."

"Right, Nick," said Mandy. "It was probably fake -- some guy in a monkey suit."

Nick shook his head. "It sure *looked* real. . . and there have been a *lot* of sightings all over northern California. How could that many people be faking it?"

Mandy sighed. Why was Nick so hung up on Bigfoot? She didn't want him scaring the little kids. And she *really* hoped he was wrong. These woods were not like the ones in the state of Maine where she lived. These trees were huge and mysterious. *Anything* could live here. "So what about your story, Nick? Are you going to tell us the rest?" Anything to get his mind off Bigfoot, Mandy thought.

"Oh, yeah," said her cousin. "Let's see – where was I? So this man, James Marshall, was helping Mr. Sutter build a sawmill on the American River. They were enlarging the ditch where the water drains away from
the waterwheel. James Marshall looked in the water and saw something shiny. He picked out four or five pieces of this bright yellowish rock. At first, he didn't even know what it was, but after he tested it, he found out it was--"

"Gold!" Christianne shouted. "It was gold, wasn't it?"

"You're right, it was," her brother said. "That was the start of the California Gold Rush in 1849. That's why the prospectors were called forty-niners."

"Oh!" said Noah. "The 49ers? That's the name of the San Francisco football team!"

Nick nodded. "The Gold Rush changed San Francisco from a small settlement to a boomtown where thousands of people lived."

"What's a prospector?" his sister asked.

"Someone who searched for gold," Nick replied, "either by digging it out of the ground or finding it in a stream or river."

"Are we going to find gold too?" Christianne asked, jumping up and down. "I saw a stream over by the camp store. We can look for gold nuggets!"

"Sit down," Nick ordered, "before you fall in the fire! Actually, I was thinking we could try panning for gold, if we can get some equipment."

"There's a frying pan in the cabin!" Christianne said, bouncing up again, ready to go get it. "Mom just used it to make supper."

Nick snorted. "Silly, you don't hunt for gold with a frying pan. You need a special type of pan with no handle. I saw some in that museum we went to in San Francisco."

Mandy put up her hand to silence them. "Do you hear something?" she said in a low voice.

A snuffling sound came from the bushes and then the crackle of small branches breaking. The children stared at each other with round eyes.

"Maybe it's a raccoon," whispered Noah, ". . . looking for a toasted marshmallow?"

"I think it's something bigger," Mandy whispered back.

A terrible smell floated around them on the breeze, making them gag.

"Nick, did you *have* to?" said Christianne, holding her nose.

"Hey, it's not me!" he protested.

"Eeuw," said Mandy. "It smells like dirty diapers times ten!"

"There's only one thing that smells like that," murmured Nick. "Sasquatch."

"Fast-squash?" asked his sister, still holding her nose. "What's that?"

"Sas-squatch," Nick repeated more slowly. "That's another name for Bigfoot."

Christianne stared at him. "Bigfoot? Here? For real?"

The bushes rustled and cracked.

"Ru-u-un!" they all yelled.

Chapter 2. A Mysterious Visitor

"Is something wrong?" asked Aunt Ariel, as the children stampeded into the cabin. She was just putting the clean frying pan into the dish drainer beside the sink.

Nick, the last one in, slammed the screen door and pushed the hook into the little loop to lock it.

"Bigfoot tried to get us, Mom!" Christianne said. "He was really big and hairy and smelled yucky!"

"Did you actually see something?" her father asked, looking up from the sports magazine he was reading at the kitchen table.

"Wel-l-l-l. . . no-o-o," the little girl said. "But we heard him and smelled him. Nick said--"

"Nick?" their father said in a sharp tone. "Have you been scaring your sister with silly stories again?"

"Uh-uh. . . I . . ." Nick stuttered, his face turning red.

"Uncle Ross," said Mandy, trying to head off trouble. "Nick was actually telling us all about the Gold Rush. He did mention there have been sightings of Bigfoot in California. When we heard noises, we thought it would be safer to come inside."

"The mosquitoes were getting bad, anyway," added Noah, waving his hands around his head. "It's a good thing the bats are out. They each eat 600 mosquitoes an hour!"

"Hmm, that's good to know, Noah," said Uncle Ross.

"No more going outside alone after dark," Aunt Ariel said, drying her hands. "We thought you'd be okay right by the cabin, but maybe not. Bears are notorious for raiding campsites. If they're hungry enough, who knows what they'll do?"

"Off to bed with you now," Uncle Ross said, with a shooing motion. "This is supposed to be a restful vacation, so give us a few moments of peace. Before I can relax, I'll have to go put out the campfire."

The four children headed to their room. Two sets of bunk beds against opposite walls were ready with sleeping bags and pillows.

"I get the top bunk!" yelled Christianne, starting to climb up the ladder.

"No way," said her brother. "Mom says she wants the 'little kids' on the bottom bunks in case they fall out of bed." He snickered. "Too bad."

Christianne squinted at him. "I bet you made that up."

"Go ask. . . if you dare," Nick replied, starting up the other ladder.

"Uh . . . never mind," said his sister, plopping down on the bottom bunk.

They took turns changing into pajamas and brushing their teeth in the one small bathroom.

"Be sure you check inside your sleeping bag before you get in," Noah suggested.

"Check for what?" Mandy asked.

"Spiders, snakes," he replied.

Mandy froze. "*Snakes*?"

"Yeah, California has *lots* of snakes. There's the gopher snake, the racer, the king snake. . . and then there are the poisonous ones – the northern Pacific rattlesnake, the western diamond-back rattlesnake, the speckled rattlesnake, the sidewinder--"

"Stop!" Mandy interrupted. "No one told me California is full of snakes! I want to go home!"

"It's okay, Mandy," said Christianne. "I'll check your sleeping bag for you." She scooted up the ladder and raised the covers. "All clear."

Nick snorted. "What did you expect, Mandy? California is next door to Nevada – lots of snakes there, as you know."

"Yeah, but at least you can see where you're stepping in Nevada. There's no grass to hide things." Mandy noticed that Nick checked his own sleeping bag, actually pulling it off the bed and shaking it . . . just in case. "Since you're so brave, Nick, you'll just have to be the leader of our expeditions. If there's a snake out there, you'll be the first to step on it."

He stopped what he was doing and stared at her. What could he say to that? "Gee, thanks," he muttered.

"Hey, I brought everyone a present," Mandy said, digging through her backpack. She pulled out a plastic bag containing four small flashlights. "Dad got them on sale, two for a dollar." She handed a blue one to Christianne and a red one to Noah. "Here's yours, Nick." She tossed one to him up on the top bunk. Then she turned off the overhead light, snapped on her flashlight and climbed the ladder to her bunk.

"Wow, this is really bright for such a small light," Christianne said, pointing it up at her brother's face across the room. "Thanks, Mandy!"

"Ouch! Cut it out, Christianne!" Nick said, shielding his eyes.

"I figured they would come in handy for exploring," Mandy replied. "They're LED lights so they should last a long time."

"Maybe for once we won't get caught in the dark with no light," said Nick. "Remember the lighthouse in Maine, that scary tunnel in New Hampshire, the creepy ghost mine in Nevada?"

"Hey," said Mandy, "*I* had a light – most of the time. Anyway, everyone has their own light now, so we should be all set."

The children crisscrossed each other's light beams on the ceiling.

"We shouldn't wear them out," said Nick, turning his off. "So what do you want to do tomorrow?"

Noah shut his light off too. "We were going to check out the camp store, remember? To see if they have what we need to pan for gold."

"And we can look in the stream," added Christianne. "Maybe we'll see something shiny, just like that James Marshall guy."

"There are lots of cool trails we can hike on," Mandy suggested. "In the camp brochure I read about a really big tree called The Old Prospector that's hollow inside. You can walk right in."

"Sounds like a plan – we'll do all three," said Nick.

The girls clicked off their flashlights and everyone snuggled down into their sleeping bags. Through the open screen window, the sounds of the night forest filtered in – the creaking branches, the low hoo-hoo of another hunting owl, the creech-creech of crickets.

Mandy was almost asleep when she heard a sound that made her eyes pop open. Something was scratching on the outside wall of the cabin. What could it be? A tree branch moving in the breeze? A raccoon looking for food? She gulped. A *bear trying to get in*?

"Hey," she whispered. "Does anyone else hear that?"

No answer. The others were already asleep.

The scratching sounded closer.

Mandy stared at the window. In the moonlight outside, a dark shape moved. Because of the screen, she couldn't make out what it was. She slipped her mini light from under her pillow and snapped it on. Taking a deep breath, she aimed it at the window.

Two shiny spots glowed behind the screen. *Eyes!*

Mandy yelped and turned off the light. With her heart thumping, she burrowed under the covers.

The creature growled. Bushes crackled and crunched and then all was silent.

Chapter 3.   The Bear Facts

"I don't know *what* it was!" Mandy told the others the next morning. They sat at the picnic table outside the cabin, eating bowls of cereal. "It was definitely alive though. Its eyes glowed like coals in a firepit."

Nick gulped down a big spoonful of Cheerios. "I bet it was Bigfoot! He was checking us out."

Mandy glanced at Christianne and Noah across the table. They had stopped eating and stared at Nick with wide eyes. "Bigfoot doesn't exist, Nick," she said, trying to reassure them. "There are lots of real animals it could have been – a coon, a bear, a . . . a . . ." She couldn't think of anything else.

"Let's go look at the back of the cabin," Nick suggested, "and see if it left any clues behind."

The kids finished their breakfast and took the bowls to the kitchen for washing. Aunt Ariel and Uncle Ross sat at the table eating English muffins and drinking coffee, both lost in reading their books.

"We'll be right outside," Nick said to them. His parents both waved a hand without looking up.

"You lead the way, Nick," Mandy said, as they stepped outside.

Nick grinned. "Afraid a little snakie will get you?"

She frowned at him. "Not at all. It will get *you* before it can get to me!"

Nick snickered and pushed his way through the bushes that hugged the cabin. Outside their bedroom window, he stopped. "Whoa, look at that!" Nick said, pointing at the wall.

Long vertical furrows scored the boards on both sides of the window.

"I *knew* I heard something scratching against the cabin!" Mandy exclaimed. "What could it be? And don't say Bigfoot!"

Noah spread his fingers so each rested in a groove. "I think it was a bear," he said.

"A *grizzly* bear?" Christianne asked, her eyes wide. "The flag in front of the camp store has a big bear on it."

"There used to be grizzlies in California, but not anymore," Noah explained. "The last one was seen in 1924. That is a grizzly on the state's flag though. They were big and blonde and powerful and had a hump on their shoulders. Lots of California teams are named after the grizzly, like the California University Golden Bears. There are still lots of regular bears."

"What does a *regular* bear look like?" Christianne asked.

"Well, they're black bears," replied Noah, "but in California, most of them are brown."

"Huh?" said Nick. "That doesn't make sense."

Noah shrugged. "That's what it says on Wikipedia."

"We have black bears in Maine," Mandy said, "and they really are black. We have a team, too – the University of Maine Black Bears. I heard black bears won't hurt you unless they're protecting their cubs."

"Or unless they're *really* hungry," Noah added. "In places like Yosemite National Park, campers have to keep their food in storage lockers. If bears smell food, they'll break into cars, campers and even cabins to get it."

18

"If the poor bears are hungry, we should leave some food out for them!" said Christianne.

Nick shook his head. "No, silly, don't you get it? If you give them food, the bears will keep coming back for more. They'll get braver around people and more dangerous!"

Christianne kicked him. "I'm not silly! You're the one carrying food around in your pants." She pointed at the granola bar sticking out of his back pocket.

Her brother danced around, holding his shin. "Grrr," he said, growling like a bear, "I'll get you for this."

"Come on, you guys, let's check out the camp store," Mandy said. "You first, Fearless Leader." She stepped aside so Nick could lead the way.

He scowled at her and then limped along the side of the cabin. At the front, he hobbled up the steps to the porch and opened the screen door. "We're going to the store," he told his parents.

Mandy smirked when she saw Nick turn his back and sneak the granola bar out of his pocket. He left it on the kitchen countertop. He had decided not to be 'bear bait' after all. She slipped on her small green backpack that contained her flashlight, money, and sweatshirt.

Her collection of key chains attached to the zipper pull jingled and jangled. Maybe she could find a new one at the store to buy as a California souvenir.

The camp store was a dark brown log cabin with steps leading up to a wide porch. Animal sculptures that looked like they had been carved from logs with a chain saw decorated the front yard.

"That must be a grizzly!" said Christianne, pointing to a life-size carving of a bear standing on its hind legs, its mouth open in a fierce snarl. She poked it in the belly with her finger. "You don't scare *me*, bear!"

Her brother rolled his eyes. "It's just a block of wood, Christianne. Come on." He led the way into the store.

Rustic wooden shelves held camping and fishing supplies and food. Up above on the walls hung the heads of *real* wild animals – a mountain lion, a wild boar, a bighorn sheep, a mule deer, a red fox, and a bear.

Several families wandered around, picking up groceries and camping gear. An old man with a bushy gray beard hovered over the fishing lures. A long-haired teen with holes in the knees of his jeans lounged against the counter with a bottle of soda in his hand.

The four children cruised up and down the aisles.

"Here's just what we need!" said Noah, pointing to a box on the shelf. "The Gold Rush Panning Kit." He peered at the writing on the box. "It's got a 12-inch pan, glass vial, snifter bottle, one-pound bag of pay dirt and a certificate of au – au. . ."

"That's au-then-ti-ci-ty," said Mandy, reading the box over his shoulder. "It means it's real. How much does it cost?"

"$39.95," Noah replied. "We don't have that much money, do we?"

"Maybe we don't need all that stuff," said Mandy, looking down the row at all the gold-hunting equipment. There were metal pans and plastic ones of different sizes. Next to them were buckets and funnels and glass containers. "We sure don't need to buy dirt. What's the point of that?" She studied the price tags. "If we put our money together, we could probably buy a couple of these plastic pans. They're $9.99 each. But we don't even know how to use them."

Overhearing the children talking, the tall young man with thick black hair who tended the cash register stuck his head around the end of the row. "Turn on the video in the corner there and you'll see how to pan for gold," he said. "It gives you step-by-step directions."

The kids crowded around the screen and Nick pressed the 'play' button. They watched a man standing in a rushing stream dig between the tree roots with a shovel. He scooped some of the gravel into his red plastic pan so it was ¾ full. He swished it around just below the surface of the water and some of the lighter stuff washed out. Keeping the side of the pan with ridges, called riffles, away from him, he continued to move the pan in a smaller circle, explaining that any gold sinks to the bottom of the pan because it's heavier. The other heavier sediment is black magnetite which can be removed with a magnet. He showed how at the end you use very small swirls to see any gold dust on the bottom of the pan. A few glints winked in the pan. "Eureka!" the man said with a smile.

Christianne squinted at the screen. "That gold is awful small. How do you get it out of the pan?"

The black-haired guy spoke up again. "Come over here and I'll show you." At the front counter he had a pan with some sediment in it. "I'm Blake, by the way."

"Hi, Blake," said Nick. "I'm Nick. This is my sister Christianne, my cousin Mandy from Maine and our friend Noah from Florida."

"Glad to meet you," said Blake with a friendly smile. "This is my pal Mogee," he added, nodding at the teen with the holey pants.

The boy peered at them from beneath floppy brown hair and lifted a limp hand in greeting.

"Now, this is a snifter," Blake said, showing them a small plastic bottle. "When you squeeze the bottle and then slowly let it out again, the sucking tube will pick up the gold dust."

"Like a little vacuum cleaner!" Christianne said, clapping her hands.

"So what do we actually need to pan for gold?" Nick asked the store-keeper. "Obviously, we need a pan, a magnet. . ."

"And a sniffer!" said Christianne.

Nick shook his head. "It's not a sniffer, silly, it's a *snifter.*"

She frowned at him. "It sniffs up the gold doesn't it? So it's a *sniffer.*"

"Whatever," he mumbled. "So how much does it cost for all this stuff?"

Blake thought for a moment. "Well, it's $10 for a pan, $8 for a magnet, and another $10 for the" -- he smiled at Christianne – "sniffer bottle, $5 for a bucket and $10 for a small shovel."

Noah added the figures in his head. "That's even more than the gold-panning kit. We can't buy all that, can we?"

Mandy and Nick both shook their heads. Each of them had $5 for spending money.

"Guess we're out of luck," Nick said, his shoulders slumping.

"Hey, tell you what," said Blake. "I've got all the equipment. I'll lend you mine for the day. If you want to pitch in and buy another pan to share, you'll have everything you need."

"Sure!" the kids all chorused.

While Blake pulled out a cardboard box and rounded up his equipment, Mandy and Christianne walked back to the shelf of pans.

"What color do you want?" Mandy asked her cousin.

Christianne looked them over. "They don't have any purple ones. That's my favorite color. So let's get blue."

"So where's a good place to pan for gold?" Nick was asking Blake when the girls got back to the counter.

"You see this stream out here?" said the store-keeper, nodding toward the front of the store. "Follow the trail to the Old Prospector, the biggest redwood tree in the park—there's a sign there -- and just beyond that where you come out of the woods, the stream widens out. Find a spot where the water is about six inches deep. You can sit on a log or rock. Oh, and you'll need to bring a small jar or pill bottle to put your gold in."

"Do you think we'll really find some?" Christianne asked.

He winked at her. "Sure you will, if you keep at it long enough. There's probably gold dust in every stream in northern California."

"Oh, boy!" the little girl said. "We're gonna be rich! Come on, guys, let's go!"

Nick's attention had been caught by a display at the end of the counter. On a rack were several DVDs, books, postcards and bumper stickers, all featuring Bigfoot.

"Hey, Blake, have *you* seen Bigfoot?" Nick asked.

The good-natured grin left the young man's face. He hesitated. "Well. . . maybe. I've caught glimpses of something when I'm leaving the store at night, a dark shape moving in the woods. I have to confess it makes me a little nervous. The reason I'm thinking it *might* be Bigfoot is because of the smell. Once in awhile the odor is just horrific, worse than a pile of sweaty socks." He wrinkled his nose at the thought. "Anyway, there are four of you – you'll be okay out in the woods in the daytime. I wouldn't go out at night though."

Nick gulped. "Uh, thanks for the warning."

"And thanks for lending us the equipment," said Mandy. "We'll bring it back before dark." She looked at Nick. "*Definitely* before dark."

Chapter 4. The Old Prospector

"Wow! Look at this tree!" exclaimed Noah. "It's a monster! 'The Old Prospector, 320 feet tall, 15 feet in diameter, 1400 years old,'" he read from the sign.

After stopping by the cabin to pack some lunches and to tell the grown-ups where they were headed, the children followed the signs along the trail to the park's biggest tree.

Mandy and Christianne set down the cardboard box of gold panning equipment they had been carrying between them. All four children tipped their heads back to look up at the gigantic redwood. They couldn't even see the top of it.

"Man, how can trees grow this tall?" Nick asked.

Noah's face scrunched in thought. "So if it's 1400 years old and this is 2014, that means the Old Prospector started growing in. . . um. . . the year 614."

"What was going on in the world then?" Mandy asked. "That was long before the United States became a country."

They looked at each other with blank expressions. They had no idea what was going on in history that far back.

"Maybe that's when T-rex was king of the world?" Christianne suggested.

Nick snorted. "No way. The dinosaurs lived millions of years ago, not hundreds."

"It was a good guess though, Christianne," Mandy said, frowning at Nick. She didn't like it when he put down his little sister.

She followed the path around to the other side of the tree. "Come see this!" she exclaimed. Mandy pulled her flashlight out of her backpack and turned it on. As the other children crowded behind her, she stepped into a big hollow in the redwood. The space was big enough for all four of them to stand inside with room left over.

"It looks like there was a fire in here," Nick said. The wood, rough and charred, was streaked with green moss. "Why would someone set a tree on fire?"

"Maybe it got hit by lightning," said Noah. "It's probably the tallest thing around. Lightning would be attracted to it."

"True," said Nick. "Does anyone know why it's called the Old Prospector?"

"I do," said Mandy. "When I was looking at the camp's map of trails yesterday, I saw some information about the tree. It said an old prospector actually lived in here back during the Gold Rush."

"It would make a great playhouse!" said Christianne. "We could put a table here and a couch over there." She pointed to likely spots. "And a refrigerator there."

Nick sniggered. "A refrigerator? Oh, and maybe an indoor pool over there and an air conditioner up there?" He pointed above them.

His sister kicked him in the knee.

"Ouch, ouch," Nick said, hopping around. He tried to catch his balance by grabbing onto the tree, but a chunk of wood broke off in his hand. Ooomph! He fell to the ground.

"I'll get you, you little rugrat," he threatened his sister, as he sat up and brushed dried redwood needles off his clothes.

"I can see why the prospector lived here," Noah said. "It's the most awesome tree house ever. I wonder if he left anything behind?"

Mandy was still moving her light around the inside walls of the tree. "Hey, what's that?" she said, holding the light steady on the spot where Nick had broken the wood away. "It looks like a shelf." She started to reach into the space and then stopped. Remembering Noah's list of California snakes, she decided it wouldn't be smart to stick her hand in a dark hole. "Uh, could you shine your lights over here?"

Christianne and Noah added their light beams to hers.

"This was hidden by the piece of wood you grabbed, Nick," Mandy said.

A stub of candle stood upright on the shelf in a puddle of hardened wax drippings. Beside it was a small tin box with a picture on the lid of a woman in an old-fashioned dress.

"Cool. I bet those belonged to the prospector!" said Nick. He took the box down from the shelf. He shook it and something rattled inside. "Shine your lights here. I think you're right, Noah. The prospector *did* leave something behind!"

"Maybe it's a big piece of gold!" his sister said. She stood so close, her nose was almost on top of the box.

"Back up, Christianne," her brother ordered. "Give me a little room." He tried wiggling the cover, but it didn't budge. "It's stuck," he murmured.

"Try this," said Noah, offering Nick a bottle opener. "I bought it at the store for my Dad because he collects them. It has Bigfoot on it."

Nick used it to pry up the edge of the cover, moving it along so the lid would raise up evenly. "I think it's working!" said Nick, excitement in his voice. With a sudden twang, the lid flew off, hitting his sister in the face.

"Ow!" said Christianne, stumbling back and grabbing Nick's arm to stop herself from falling.

"Hey!" Nick shouted, thrown off balance. He dropped the box.

"Are you all right, Christianne?" Mandy asked in concern.

The little girl rubbed her nose and glared at her brother. "You did that on purpose, didn't you, Nick?"

"No, it was an accident," he replied. "But I could say something about sticking your nose in where it doesn't belong!"

"Don't be mean, Nick," Mandy said, hands on hips. "We *all* wanted to see what's in the box."

Nick frowned at her. "Yeah, but--"

"Hey, you guys, cut it out," Noah said in his quiet voice. "Don't you want to see what *was* in the box?" He held his hands behind his back.

They all crowded around him.

"Do you have it?" Mandy asked.

"What is it?" Nick said.

"Is it gold?" Christianne asked, her eyes shining.

Noah held out one hand and slowly opened it. On his palm was a small rusty piece of metal.

"All right!" said Mandy. "The prospector had a key!"

"Oh, boy!" said Christianne. "What do you think it goes to?"

Nick traded glances with Mandy, their argument forgotten. "With every key comes a mystery," he said. "A mystery for us to solve."

Mandy nodded. "First there was the old lightkeeper's key that Papa Gene gave me, then the key we found in the model ship's carved wooden man."

Nick jumped in. "And the old miner's key on the dog skeleton's collar--"

Christianne held up her hand. "*And* the key in the telescope at The Crow's Nest Inn."

"They all led to treasure of *some* kind," said Mandy. "Maybe not gold and jewels, but interesting stuff from the past."

They all stared at the key in Noah's hand.

"Maybe this time it will be *real* treasure," Christianne whispered, saying what all of them were thinking.

Chapter 5. The Prospector's Key

"It's kind of a boring key," Christianne said, still peering into Noah's hand. "It doesn't *look* like it would go to a treasure chest."

The key was only two inches long. It had a double tooth, a simple loop at the top and was reddish-brown with rust.

"You never know," said Mandy, a thoughtful look on her face. "If you think about the purpose of keys, it's usually to protect something valuable."

"Or to keep someone in or someone out," added Nick.

"So what's in your other hand?" Christianne asked Noah.

The little boy opened his left hand in front of him. He held a piece of yellowish paper, folded into a small rectangle.

"Wow, maybe it's a note from the old prospector!" said Nick, reaching for the paper.

"Be careful, don't tear it," Mandy warned. "Let's sit on the ground so we can open it out flat."

The four children sat in a circle on the floor of the tree cave.

Nick slowly opened the paper, spreading it out. The old paper was about 2 inches tall and 3 inches wide with rips in some of the creases.

Mandy shined her light on it. It seemed to be a drawing done in pencil of some random shapes. She pointed at a squiggle. "That looks like a tree."

"It might be *this* tree, the Old Prospector!" Noah exclaimed. "What do you think *that* is?" He pointed at another wiggly line on the paper.

Christianne said, "It's wavy like water. I bet it's the stream!"

"That looks like a cabin," said Nick, touching the drawing. "But after all this time, I doubt if it's still standing."

Mandy's eyebrows scrunched up in thought. She pointed to a group of four cylinder shapes. "What about this? A bunch of batteries?"

"Did they have batteries back then?" Noah asked.

Nick shrugged. "I doubt it. Maybe they're logs or mini Tootsie Rolls. Who knows?"

Christianne sat back with a sigh. "There's no X marks the spot. It can't be a treasure map."

Noah shook his head. "The old prospector kept this piece of paper so it must have been important to him. Don't give up yet."

"Noah's right," Mandy said. She handed her light to Christianne and carefully refolded the paper. She noticed some faint writing on the back side of the drawing. "Hey, look at this," she said, opening the paper again. "It looks like a poem." She squinted to try to make out the words and then read them aloud.

"I labored long and hard for gold,
In many years of trying,
But when I took it brave and bold,
I left some others crying."

"Hmm," said Nick. "It sure sounds like a prospector wrote it. It is hard work looking for gold. But what does he mean about taking it? Did he jump someone's claim?"

"Who knows?" Mandy replied. "It seems like he would have kept some money in his tin box if he had any. We'll keep this. Since the hiding place is open now, we can't put it back there. Someone else might take it." She slid it into her pocket.

"Let's get going," said Nick. "I want to try panning for gold in the stream."

"Me, too! Me, too!" Christianne and Noah said, jumping to their feet.

They ducked through the opening in the tree and gathered up their gear.

Mandy unzipped a small compartment on her backpack. "I think the drawing might be safer in here."

"Wait, Mandy," said Noah, holding out his hand. "Take the key and tin box too. I wouldn't want to lose them."

Mandy put the drawing and the key back in the tin box. She dropped the box into her pack. "Thanks, Noah."

Nick clutched the cardboard box of equipment in his arms and shifted from foot to foot. "Come on, guys, let's get going. The day's not getting any younger. There's gold a-waiting!"

They tramped down the winding path with Nick in the lead. Wisps of mist floated through the tall trees like a gathering of ghostly forms. The fog seemed to dampen the normal sounds of the forest, making it unnaturally quiet.

"It's kind of creepy," said Christianne in a loud whisper, glancing around nervously. "Are you sure there aren't any grizzly bears?"

"They're extinct, remember?" Noah whispered too. "There aren't any left in California. . . um, at least that's what they say."

"Why do you say that?" Mandy, who was right behind him, asked.

"Um, because I think there's something following us." He kept on walking, but nodded his head at a big tree off to their right.

Startled, Mandy glanced in that direction in time to see a dark shape glide from one tree to another. She blinked. Did she really see something or was it her imagination?

"Wouldn't a bear make more noise?" Mandy said to Noah in a low voice. "And why would it follow us?"

Noah shrugged and kept on walking. He kept glancing at the trees. His shoulders were hunched like he expected something to jump out at them.

Mandy breathed a sigh of relief when the trail led them out of the foggy forest and into the bright morning sunshine. The stream, sparkling and splashing over rocks like happy music, meandered beside the path. "Yes," she said under her breath. She felt a lot safer out in the open.

"Okay," called Nick from the lead, "look for a good spot."

"How about right there?" Noah suggested, pointing at a rounded stone up the stream about twenty feet away. "I'd say the water is about six inches deep there."

Nick set down the box on the path. "Looks good to me." He pulled out a red plastic pan.

They all sat down to take off their sneakers.

Christianne stooped over the box and took out the blue pan. "Girls can share and boys can share. We'll find our own spot, won't we, Mandy?"

"You bet," said Mandy. She glanced around and pointed to a rock a few yards away from the boys'. "How about that one?"

"Okay," Christianne replied. "Can I go first?"

"Sure, come on." Mandy waded out to the rock, the water swirling around her bare feet. The stone, worn smooth by the constantly moving water, was big enough so they could both sit on it.

Nick and Noah settled on their own perch. Nick dipped the pan deep into the water and scooped up sediment from the bottom. Holding the pan so the side with the riffles was closest to him, he began to swirl it around.

Christianne struggled with her pan. Filled with water and dirt, it was heavy for her small hands to keep a grip on. As she tried to lift it above the surface, it slipped and fell back down.

After the same thing happened several times, she emptied the pan and handed it to Mandy. "You go first," she said. "Maybe if I watch you, I'll see how to do it. First I need a drink. All this water is making me thirsty." She sloshed her way back to the stream bank.

"Would you get a bottle of water for me, too?" Mandy called to her cousin.

"Where did Nick put the cardboard box?" Christianne yelled above the rushing water. She searched through the long grass and under the bushes.

The box was gone.

Chapter 6. A Thief Strikes

"That's impossible," said Nick, wading to the shore. "The box was right here a few minutes ago. I should know – I was the one carrying it." He looked around, even though his sister had already searched the area.

"How could something disappear that fast?" Christianne demanded. "Nick, did you hide it somewhere?"

"No, silly, why would I do that?"

Brother and sister glared at each other.

Mandy and Noah, who had waded to shore to see what was going on, exchanged glances.

"Uh, wait a minute, guys," Mandy said. "In the woods Noah and I saw a moving shape in the trees. We thought it might be something following us, but we weren't sure. It was hard to see with all that fog."

"Maybe that was the thief," said Noah. "Would a bear carry a box?"

"Not likely," said Nick. "It would just tear into the food. . . but Bigfoot might take it."

"That's crazy," Mandy protested. "How could a huge creature like that be right here and we not see it? Besides, Bigfoot doesn't exist!"

"Maybe it was a person," Christianne suggested. "If so, I'm pretty mad at him. He took my lunch!"

Nick had been thinking. "We're in worse trouble than that. All of Blake's gold-panning equipment was in that box, except for the pan. He trusted us to take care of it."

"And we don't have enough money to replace it," said Mandy. "We'll just have to find it!" She started looking around the shore for clues.

"I'm really thirsty," Christianne said. "I'll get a drink from the stream." She waded back into the water and scooped some in her cupped hands.

"I wouldn't, Christianne," Noah said. "There might be parasites in the water that will make you sick."

"Parasites? What's that?" she asked.

"They're little animals that are so small you can only see them with a microscope. They can give you 'beaver fever'," Noah explained, "which is usually an upset stomach, diarrhea and lots of stinky gas. I read about it in a book about camping. People think streams in the wilderness are clean, but they forget that animals, and sometimes people, uh . . . do their business in them."

"Do their business?" Christianne repeated, puzzled.

"You know," Nick said. "What you do on the toilet. . . number 2!"

Christianne stared at the water in her hands, as if seeing nasty little creatures swimming there. "Eeuww." She dumped it back in the stream and wiped her hands on her pants. She couldn't get out of the stream fast enough.

Nick snickered. "Thanks for not drinking the water," he said to his sister. "It's smelly enough around here without you adding king-size stink bombs." He held his nose and waved his other hand in front of his face.

She frowned at him, her mouth in a tight line.

As she attempted to kick him, he dodged her and stepped on a wobbly rock. "Hey!" he protested. He tried to catch his balance, but fell backward into the stream with a gigantic splash. He sat in the water, glaring at his sister. Drops dribbled down his face. "You're in big trouble, rugrat," he growled.

Christianne stuck out her tongue at him. "Did you swallow any water? We don't want to be around when *you* start making stinkies. They would probably make the whole world blow up!"

Nick growled again and picked himself up. His wet clothes stuck to his skin. When he got to the bank, he headed toward his sister, his hands raised and his face snarling like a grizzly bear.

She dashed behind Mandy for protection.

As Nick tried to reach past Mandy to grab Christianne, Mandy raised her hand to stop him. "Wait," she said. "Look at this." She pointed to a bush beside her.

A clump of reddish-brown fur was stuck in the prickly branches.

"I was looking for footprints and found this. What kind of animal do you think it came from?"

The children gathered around the bush, the fight forgotten.

"Maybe a beaver?" Noah suggested. "No, forget that. It's too far off the ground. . . It's too high up for a fox, too."

"Maybe it *was* a bear that was following us," Mandy said. "It smelled the food and waited until it could snatch it."

Nick snorted. "Come on. It took the whole box! We already agreed a bear wouldn't do that." His eyes narrowed. "No, there's only one thing it could be. That fur is the exact color of Bigfoot's hair."

Mandy crossed her arms. She did *not* want to believe in Bigfoot. It was too crazy and, well. . . too scary. She hated the thought of huge hairy creatures, half ape, half human, skulking around in the woods watching them. Obviously, *Nick* wanted to believe that. What was wrong with the guy, anyway? "There's got to be another explanation," she said.

"Face the truth, Mandy!" Nick said in exasperation. "What else could it be?"

She ignored his question and sat down to put her sneakers on. Then she started looking around for more clues. She noticed the little kids were staying close. Nick's repeated mentions of Bigfoot would probably give them nightmares. What if he was right? What if Bigfoot *was* real? So many people had seen him, they couldn't all be making it up – could they? Whatever had taken the box, had to be able to walk upright to carry it. That narrowed it down to a bear, a person or. . . Bigfoot.

"Pee-yoo," said Christianne, squeezing her nose shut. "Nick, you *did* swallow some stream water, didn't you? You must have gotten 'beaver fever'!"

"It's not me!" he protested.

The odor of week-old garbage wafted around them, getting stronger by the minute.

"Eeu-u-uw!" they all yelled.

"Bigfoot is back!" shouted Nick. "Let's get out of here!"

Chapter 7. Strange Evidence

The kids thundered down the path and into the woods like a spooked herd of wild horses.

"Wait!" cried Mandy, stopping short.

The others stopped too, panting hard.

"What is it?" Nick asked. "What did you see?" He gasped for breath and his eyes darted around the forest, searching for a menacing figure.

"That's just the point," said Mandy. "I didn't see anything and neither did you. We need to go back to the stream."

Nick stared at her. "Huh? Are you crazy? Bigfoot is back there! We might not have seen him, but we sure smelled him!"

"There's no such thing," Mandy said. "There's got to be another reason. We need to find out what's going on."

"Mandy's right," said Noah. "Plus we left the pans behind. We lost all of Blake's equipment – the least we can do is bring back his pan."

"And ours!" Christianne chimed in. "We paid $10 for that pan. We can't leave it for Bigfoot to eat his dinner out of!"

Nick moaned. "You guys *are* crazy!" He crossed his arms. "So go ahead, but I'm waiting right here."

"Come on, Nick," Mandy protested. "We need to stay together." She looked at the tall trees around them. Tatters of fog still floated among them like hovering ghosts. "Besides, it would be creepy in the woods by yourself. Who knows what might be lurking here, waiting to pounce on someone all alone. . . an unsuspecting victim?" She knew she was laying it on thick, but she didn't care. Someone, or some*thing*, had taken the box. They were safer if they stuck together.

"Whatever," Nick mumbled, his mouth in a stubborn line.

Mandy started back toward the stream. The little kids followed, glancing back at Nick. Just as the trail curved around a huge redwood, cutting off their view of him, she heard scurrying behind them.

Nick rounded the corner and caught up with them. "Uh, I decided you might need my help."

Holding back the grin that wanted to break out, Mandy managed to keep a straight face. Her strategy worked. She wouldn't admit it to Nick, but she was relieved he had decided to stay with them.

In a few moments, they arrived back at the place where they had been panning for gold. The grass on the stream bank, well-trampled from their search for the box, was empty.

"Uh, oh," said Christianne. "The pans are gone too! Weren't they right here on this rock?"

"Yeah, I set mine down there to hunt for the box," Nick said.

"And I stacked mine on top of yours," Mandy said.

"Do you think they got knocked off and fell in the water?" asked Noah, looking over the side. "They're plastic, so they should float." He peered down the stream, looking for a spot of blue or red.

"Maybe they're caught in the weeds or something," Mandy said. "Let's follow the water." She took off her sneakers again. Staying close to the shore, she waded downstream.

"I'll keep following the path," Nick called out, "in case the thief dropped anything."

Noah followed Nick, and Christianne trailed after Mandy.

"What do you think is going on?" Christianne asked her cousin. "How could all our stuff just disappear?"

"It couldn't," Mandy replied, "not by itself." She lifted low branches that trailed in the water, searching for the pans.

"This is turning into a real mystery," Christianne said, peering behind a big rock. "Do you think we can figure it out?"

"We've *got* to," Mandy said, a desperate note in her voice. She stopped for a moment, her hands on her hips. "We can't pan for gold without the pans. *Plus* Blake will never trust us again if we don't find his equipment. Your Mom and Dad will have to pay for it and they'll be upset that we were so irresponsible. They'll probably ground us and we'll have to stay with them every minute of the day. Our vacation will be ruined!"

They continued down the stream.

Christianne made her way around another big boulder. "Hey," she said, "look at this!" She reached down into a pool between two rocks and picked something up. She waded over to Mandy and held out a torn piece of colored paper.

"What is it?" Mandy asked.

"It's the wrapper of a power bar. . . the same kind I put in my lunch bag!"

Mandy took it from her and studied it for a moment. "Yeah, I had one too. It could be a coincidence. Probably Aunt Ariel bought them at the camp store. That means anyone from around here could have dropped it."

Christianne's eyes narrowed. "Maybe," she said, "but maybe not. I'm thinking whoever stole our lunch started eating it as they walked along the path and threw the wrapper in the water!"

"Well, a bear sure wouldn't peel off the paper. It would just eat the whole thing."

"What about Bigfoot?" Christianne asked, her eyes wide now.

Mandy snorted. "I have no idea how Bigfoot eats things. It doesn't really matter since he isn't real." *I hope*, she added silently.

Just then they heard an excited voice. "Hey, Mandy, Christianne, over here!"

"Nick found something. Come on!" Christianne said.

The girls walked through the water and scrambled up onto the shore.

"Where are you guys?" Mandy called.

"Down here!" Nick shouted. "Follow the trail."

Christianne and Mandy jogged along the path. They found the boys bending over something.

"What is it?" Mandy panted.

The boys each took a step sideways so the girls could see what they were looking at. On the ground, impressed an inch deep into the soft mud, was a footprint. A *gigantic* footprint.

"Oh, no," Mandy murmured. She did not want to believe her eyes. It was the biggest footprint she had ever seen. It had five toes just like a human's, but was wider across the front of the foot and, of course, much longer. There weren't too many creatures that could have made it. An elephant? A hippo? Tyrannasaurus Rex?? None of which existed in a California forest.

"Bigfoot," Nick whispered. "This proves it."

Chapter 8. The Creature Lurks

Noah pulled a small tape rule out of a pocket of his hiker shorts and crouched down. He measured from the heel to the middle toe of the big footprint. "It's 14½ inches long!" He stretched the tape the other way. "And 5 inches wide. Super Size!"

Nick looked at the boy, surprised. "Do you always carry a measuring tape with you?"

"Sure," he replied. "Don't you? It sure comes in handy."

Nick shook his head and then grinned at Mandy. "What do you say now? Do you still think Bigfoot is bogus? I don't think there are any campers running around with feet this size!"

"I don't know what to think," she said, somewhat dazed. "Did you find any other prints?"

"Actually, we stopped when we saw this," Nick said. "Let's walk ahead a bit." He led the way down the trail, his eyes on the ground.

"Here's another one!" He pointed at a second perfect impression.

Noah stretched out the tape rule and measured the distance between the prints. "Wow, the footprints are 40 inches apart! That means this guy is pretty tall. That's a long way to step."

"Is it a giant?" Christianne whispered, standing close to Mandy. "Will he say 'fee, fie, foe, fum' and gobble us up?"

Mandy put her arm around her cousin's shoulders. "I'd say he'd rather eat power bars and PBJs!" She pointed at a plastic sandwich bag on the edge of the path streaked with peanut butter and strawberry jam.

Christianne crossed her arms. "He *did* steal my lunch! See, I drew a smiley face on the bag with a marker. That proves it's mine.
He should be arrested! And he shouldn't be such a litter bug!" She picked up the baggie and scowled at it.

"Look, here's more trash," Noah said, wandering farther up the trail. He scooped up another power bar wrapper and sandwich baggie.
"Bigfoot has more than big feet – he has a big appetite!"

Mandy rested her chin in her hand with a frown on her face. "Don't you think it's strange there are two perfect footprints on the path and that's all? It's muddy in other places too."

Nick studied the ground. "The grass is trampled on the edge here, like he tried *not* to walk on the path. That *is* kind of strange. Why would he care?"

"Maybe he doesn't like getting his big feet all muddy," suggested Christianne.

"Or for some reason he didn't want to leave more footprints," said Noah. "Maybe he doesn't want us following him."

Mandy snorted. "Too bad. We're *going* to follow him and we're *going* to get our stuff back!" She stalked down the path with her hands clenched.

The others marched along behind.

"What about snakes?" Nick called after her.

Mandy stopped short and the others crashed into each other like a line of dominoes. "Why did you have to say that?" she said, whirling around and stabbing a finger at Nick. "*You* lead!"

Nick's snickers only made Mandy madder. She could see why Christianne was always kicking him. She felt like kicking him too. He could be *so* annoying.

Just then he stopped. "Whoa, something happened here!" he said, stepping aside so they could see.

Just beyond a rocky patch, a dent showed in the soft ground. Next to it lay a couple of Granny Smith apples and a lunch bag.

"I bet Bigfoot tripped and dropped the box!" said Noah. "That's *my* lunch bag. I drew a picture of Bigfoot on it."

They all stared at the drawing of a fuzzy creature with cartoon eyes and buck teeth.

Christianne picked it up. "Bigfoot should have eaten *your* lunch first since his picture was on it!" She handed it to Noah. "Can I have your power bar? I'm really hungry."

Noah opened the bag and took out the food. "I'll share."

Something shiny under a fern caught Mandy's eye. She stooped and scooped it up. "All right!" she said, holding the object on the palm of her hand for them all to see. "Blake's snifter! It must have fallen out of the box. We're definitely on the right track."

A crashing in the bushes made them all freeze.

"Oh, no," said Christianne in a small voice. "It's Bigfoot."

A low growl made the hair on the back of Mandy's neck stand up.

"We need to get out of here," Nick said in a shaky voice. His feet weren't moving.

The strong odor of rotten eggs drifted around them.

"Oh, ick!" Christianne said, holding her nose.

"Yuck," said Noah, pinching his nose shut too.

"This way," murmured Mandy, sidling further down the path, a step at a time. She had a feeling the creature wanted them to turn back, but she was determined not to run away. Her stomach fluttered with butterflies. She grabbed Christianne's hand and pulled her along with her.

Noah stuck with them. Nick was still rooted to the spot.

"Nick!" Mandy hissed. "Come on!"

Another growl came from the same place in the bushes.

Nick backed away and then stumbled after the other children. He kept glancing over his shoulder, expecting to be chased by a huge, hideous, hairy ape man with upraised claws.

"We need to hide!" Mandy said, almost flying along the path now. She noticed a faint trail branching off from the main one. "This way!" She pushed through the waist-high grass, following the narrow
route that twisted among the trees. Raspberry bushes scratched her arms. She

held them back so they wouldn't whack the little kids in the face.

"Mandy, you're going to get us lost!" Nick protested from the rear of the line. "This path hasn't been used in a hundred years!"

"Shhh, quiet," she warned over her shoulder. She faced forward to take a step and then turned to ice.

A dry, rattling sound came from the ground in front of her. Mandy's eyes widened in horror. A black and white striped snake, about four feet long, vibrated its tail. "R-r-rattle, sn-snake," she said in a quaky voice.

"Don't move," Christianne said behind her.

Mandy moaned. She wanted to close her eyes, but they seemed to be propped open in terrible fascination. In trying to escape one horrible beast, she had met the worst one of all. She had forgotten all about snakes. She had traipsed through the long grass like an idiot without a thought of what might be crawling there.

The snake gathered itself into a coil and raised its head, staring right at Mandy with its black, beady eyes. It hissed at her.

"I'm going to die," she whispered.

Chapter 9. A Warning

Noah peered around Christianne to get a look at the snake. "Don't worry, Mandy," he said. "It's not a rattlesnake."

"W-what?" she quivered. "It has to be – it's rattling its tail!"

The little boy took a step closer. "Nope. It's a king snake, one of the most common snakes in California, and it's not poisonous. I read all about it on Wikipedia. If it's in dry leaves when it vibrates its tail, it *sounds* like a rattlesnake."

Mandy still wasn't convinced. "How can you be sure it's *not* a rattlesnake?"

"Rattlesnakes don't have those colors and their heads have a different shape," said Noah. "I looked at lots of pictures."

"Noah's right," Nick said. "Remember, I've seen tons of rattlesnakes in Nevada. Here, take this." He poked Mandy in the back with a forked stick he had broken off a nearby tree. "You can pin its head down."

Mandy gave a screech and whirled around. She grabbed the stick out of Nick's hand. "What are you doing? Would you like *your* head pinned down?" She threatened him with the stick.

"Chill, Mandy," he said, fending her off. "You're so touchy. Help, Noah!"

"I'll take care of it, Mandy," Noah said. "Can I have the stick?"

"Sure," she replied, handing it to him. "I'm done leading this expedition!"

Noah prodded the black-and-white reptile with the stick. "Time to go home, King." It hissed at him but didn't budge. "Okay, you'll have to have a flying lesson then." He slid the stick under the snake and heaved it through the air. It landed some- where in the bushes off to the side.

"Awesome!" said Christianne. "I never saw a snake fly before. If it had wings it would be like a skinny dragon!"

Nick snorted. "Right. If pigs could fly."

His sister frowned in confusion. "What do pigs have to do with it?"

"Nothing. It's just a saying." He took the stick from Noah. "Come on. We might as well see where this path goes."

"Uh, I'll take over the end of the line now," said Mandy. "To make sure we all stay together."

"Right," Nick said again, a smirk on his face. He thwacked at the long grass in front of him with the stick. "Follow the leader."

"Uh, Nick?" Noah said, right behind him. "Be careful. There *could* be rattlesnakes in here."

Mandy groaned.

The faint track continued through the grassy area and back into the woods. Rather than redwoods, the trees seemed to be a mixture of birch, maple, and oak, much younger than the tall sequoias.

"Probably this used to be cleared land," said Nick, "where someone lived."

The words were no sooner out of his mouth, when they spied an old cabin. The front door hung by one hinge and a tree grew through the caved-in roof. Thick shrubs leaned against the sides of the derelict building like tired gnomes.

For some reason, it reminded Mandy of the witch's house in Hansel and Gretel. Only instead of being made of tasty gingerbread and candy, its boards were green with moss and creeping vines. It smelled of rotting wood. Mandy shuddered.

"Maybe this is Bigfoot's house," said Christianne, standing close to Mandy.

"He'd have a hard time fitting in there," Nick said. "Let's take a look."

"Wait!" Noah warned. "This is the kind of place snakes love to hang out in. Be really careful."

"I'll wait right here," Mandy said, crossing her arms.

"Me too," agreed Christianne.

Nick pushed against the crooked door. He jumped back as its one hinge gave way and the door collapsed outward with a muffled thump. He stepped onto it and peered into the dark space. "Can't see much," he muttered. "Does anyone have a light?"

"We *all* have a light," said Mandy. "Remember? Check your pocket."

"Uh, well, I didn't think I'd need it in the daytime," Nick said. "It's back at the camp."

"I've got mine!" said Christianne.

"Me too!" Noah dug his out of a compartment in his multi-pocketed shorts.

"And me," Mandy said, giving Nick a smug look.

"Whatever," Nick mumbled, holding out his hand.

Noah got there first. He slapped his little red flashlight into Nick's waiting palm and then slid in beside him.

"Three lights are better than one," Mandy said.

She and Christianne crowded into the doorway behind the boys. They both switched their lights on and swung the beams around the interior.

"I thought you were going to wait outside," Nick said over his shoulder.

"Oh, well," said Mandy, who didn't want to miss out if they found something interesting in the cabin. "You're in front so you'll scare any snakes away."

Nick turned back. "Stop the light show. You're making me dizzy. Let's start with the floor. First shine your lights in the left corner and we'll move them a little bit at a time around to the right."

They synchronized their lights and started to scan the inside of the cabin. Fallen boards partially covered the dirt floor. Something skittered out of a pile of wood and across the ground to the far corner.

Mandy gave a small shriek and leaped back. Her light rays danced on the far wall and then the ceiling.

"Chill, Mandy," said Nick, following the creature with Noah's light. "It's just a mouse."

She sucked in a big breath and let it out slowly, getting herself together. She *was* jumpy. The sooner they found the gold-panning stuff and got back to camp, the happier she would be. Thieves and Bigfoot she could deal with, but almost stepping on that gigantic snake was too much. Its evil friends could be anywhere.

"Wait," said Noah, jogging Nick's elbow. "Shine the light on the wall. I saw something when Mandy's flashlight was bouncing around."

Both Nick and Christianne pointed their lights at the wall across from them. Foot high words in red spray paint splattered the surface like blood.

"What does it say?" Christianne asked.

They all studied the wild writing.

Mandy peered over the little kids' heads. "It says 'WARNING! GO HOME OR ELSE!'"

Chapter 10. Trapped!

"Is that message for us?" Christianne asked.

Mandy's light beam dropped below the words to where something else was written in smaller red letters. She squinted, trying to make it out. "THIS MEANS YOU!" she read.

Nick shook his head. "It might *not* be meant for us. It could have been put there twenty years ago."

Noah sniffed. "Doesn't it smell like fresh paint to you?"

Everyone snuffed in the musty air of the decaying cabin.

"Now that you mention it. . ." Mandy said.

Nick backed out of the doorway. "Uh, who knew we were headed this way? *We* didn't even know!"

"Bigfoot?" Christianne said in a small voice. "He must have watched us from the bushes and got here before us."

"Yeah, right," said her brother, "and picked up a can of paint on the way to leave us a message."

They all gave a nervous laugh. The thought of Bigfoot puttzing around with spray paint did seem pretty silly.

Noah voiced what they were all thinking. "Well, if it wasn't Bigfoot, who was it?"

"And why?" Mandy added. "Why is someone trying to scare us away?" The thought made her all the more determined to *not* run away. "Maybe they're hiding something?" She took a step farther inside and waved her light around. "Come on, guys. We need to put our lights together."

Nick and Christianne squeezed in behind her and added their lights to hers.

"I'll keep watch out here in case someone comes," Noah said from the doorway. "Shout if you find anything."

The kids continued to move their lights around the room together. They had almost made a complete circle when their combined beams lit up a green tarp halfway along one wall.

"Hey, what's that?" said Mandy.

"It couldn't have been there long," said Nick. "There's no dust on it."

"Why don't you take a look?" Mandy suggested. There was no way she would lift up a tarp in a possible snake den.

"Yeah. . . okay," Nick mumbled. He took a hesitant step toward the corner.

A screech tore through the air. Something thrashed in the dark space above. It plummeted down straight at Nick.

"Ahhhh!" he yelled, thrusting up his hands to defend himself. The small flashlight sailed from his grasp, landing somewhere in the debris. It went out.

The girls screamed as the creature zoomed above them. They ducked and stayed crouched down with their hands covering their heads.

Noah heard their cries of alarm and rushed to the entrance. "Are you guys okay?"

Christianne stumbled out of the doorway. "A m-monster tried to get us! It jumped down from the ceiling!"

"A *monster*?" asked Noah. "What did it look like?"

The little girl shook her head. "I don't really know. But it was big and scary. It went out the door. Didn't you see it?"

"No, I was watching the path. Where's Mandy and Nick?"

"We're in here!" yelled Mandy. "Come and see this!"

The two children tiptoed back into the cabin. Christianne held out her flashlight like a sword, ready to fight off another monster.

"Over here," Mandy said from the corner.

"Is it. . . it safe in here?" Christianne asked, not moving from the entrance.

"It was just an owl," Nick replied. "It must have been asleep up in the rafters and we woke it up."

"It was huge!" his sister said, her eyes as wide as the owl's. "It almost knocked me over with its gigantic wings!"

"It was probably as scared as we were," Nick said. "Anyway, look what we found. This was under the tarp."

Mandy shined her light into a cardboard box. Jumbled together were the two plastic pans, bucket, small shovel, glass jar and a magnet.

"Hey, it's our stuff!" said Christianne.

"It's mostly Blake's stuff," Noah corrected, bending over to get a better look.

"What a relief," said Mandy. She pulled the snifter out of her pocket and added it to the box. "Now we can return his equipment and Blake will never know it was missing for awhile."

"Uh, don't you think we should tell him someone stole it?" Nick asked, standing up. "It's pretty weird that someone is hanging around and grabs stuff while we're not looking. Blake might want to report it to a ranger or something."

Mandy raised an eyebrow. "So you don't think it was Bigfoot after all?"

He frowned. "Well, it doesn't seem like something Bigfoot would do. Why would he want gold-panning stuff? But we've heard him and we've smelled him so I still say he's around."

Mandy rolled her eyes. She wished he would give it up. But it wasn't worth arguing about right now. She thought for a moment and then shook her head.

"I don't think we should tell anyone about the thief, at least not yet. Uncle Ross and Aunt Ariel would be worried. We won't be allowed to go out on our own and then we'll never be able to find out who did it."

Christianne nodded. "Mandy's right. We need to solve this mystery. We'll only be here five more days, so we have to work fast."

Nick sighed. "All right. Let's get this box out of here then. Give me some light."

The girls aimed their flashlights at the box while Nick lifted it. Then they waved them in front of their feet as they headed toward the rectangle of daylight. It was slow going trying to light everyone's way so they didn't trip over boards or metal pieces.

With a slam that startled them all, the daylight disappeared. They stopped in their tracks.

"What's going on?" said Nick.

The sound of hammering came from outside.

"Uh, oh," Noah said.

Mandy fired her light beam to where the open doorway had been. The old wooden door now covered the space.

"Someone's trying to close us in," she shouted. "Come on!"

Nick dropped the box.

Stumbling and bumbling into each other, they rushed to the entrance. They pushed and pummeled on the door.

"Hey, let us out!"

No answer.

"We're trapped," Christianne whispered.

Chapter 11. Escape

Look out, everyone," Nick said, spreading his arms and backing up a few steps. "I'll get this thing open!"

The other children stepped out of the way to give him room.

Nick took a side stance and focused on the wooden door. With a mighty 'hi-*ya*,' he leaped at the obstacle and kicked it hard with the bottom of his foot. It didn't budge. He tried again and again. Then he pounded on the door with his fists. "Let us out!"

The other children joined in pounding on the door and yelling.

No answer came from outside.

Nick sagged against the door in defeat, breathing hard. "Why would anyone do this?"

"Good question," said Mandy. "We'll think about it later. Right now we need to get out of here. The place is falling down – it can't be very strong. We need to look around." Exploring the dark interior of the cabin made her skin crawl. She could only hope that the commotion had sent any rattlesnakes crawling away.

"This is scary," Christianne said, standing close to Mandy and sniffling. "I don't like it in here."

"It's okay," said Mandy, putting her arm around her. "We'll get out of here somehow. Help me with your light."

Christianne pointed her flashlight on the floor and its beam joined Mandy's, making a brighter and bigger circle of illumination.

Mandy shut her eyes for a moment and took a deep breath. Then she opened them and studied the floor in front of her feet before taking each step. The two girls slowly made their way along the wall. Every few steps, Mandy pressed on the wall, but it seemed solid.

"This must have been a window," she said, flashing her light at a crisscross of boards, "but it's covered over too." She felt a bubble of panic rising from her stomach, but she pushed it down. "There's *got* to be a way out."

"I have an idea," said Noah, who was still standing by the doorway with Nick. "Turn off the lights for a minute."

Christianne gave a small gasp. "But it will be too dark, Noah."

"No, just stay where you are for a few minutes and let your eyes get used to it. Then we'll be able to see any gaps between the boards because the daylight will shine through."

"Actually that makes sense," said Nick, finally getting his breathing under control. "We might be able to smash a hole in the wall if we find a weak spot."

Mandy wasn't thrilled about being in the dark, but she snapped off the light. Christianne did the same. They stood in the blackness, holding onto each other.

It seemed like a long time, but it was really just a couple of minutes before Mandy realized she could make out the shape of her cousin beside her. Glancing around, she noticed chinks of light where some of the boards didn't quite meet. Overhead, where the tree grew through the roof, a ragged halo surrounded the trunk.

"What do you think, Nick?" said Mandy. "Could we get through up there?" The hole was about five feet above their heads. It would have to be made much bigger for a person to get through.

Nick stood up and stared at the opening. "We need something to stand on. Turn on the light."

The girls both scanned the room with their lights, searching for something they could use to climb on. Rotting boards, an old coffee pot, and a rusty iron bed frame were the only recognizable objects in sight.

"The bed frame!" said Noah. "If we lean it up against the tree, we can use it as a ladder. Come on!"

The boys scuffed over to the dilapidated mass of metal while the girls lit their way.

Nick surveyed it, hands on hips. "It looks dangerous to me. If you're on that and it collapses, you could get stabbed by a broken bed spring. You'd be shish kebab. *I'm* not standing on it!"

"I'll do it," Noah said in a firm voice. "I don't weigh much and you can hold onto me. Help me set it up."

They grabbed opposite sides of the bed frame and struggled to place it on end against the tree trunk.

"Does anyone have a piece of rope with them?" Mandy asked.

"Yeah, sure, I have a lasso hanging right on my belt loop," Nick replied in a sarcastic tone. "I carry it with me everywhere."

Mandy scowled at him. "Don't be so cranky, Nick. I was just asking."

"I've got some paracord," Noah said, pulling a coil from his pocket. "Would that work?" He tossed it to Mandy.

She grinned at Nick while she tied the bed frame to the tree. "That will help. At least now it can't slide down. Okay, Noah, we'll give you a hand up."

Nick made a stirrup of his hands and Noah stepped into it with his right foot. After Nick had boosted him up as far as he could, he grabbed Noah's ankles to give him some support. Noah climbed a bit higher. Holding on to the tree with one hand, he reached toward the hole with the other. He pushed at the ragged edge of roof, dislodging a few loose shingles. A shower of dirt, moss and bits of dried wood rained down on them.

"Ick!" said Christianne, shaking the debris out of her hair.

"Step back a little," Nick said. "You don't have to be right under the hole." A layer of dust covered the top of his head like gray frosting.

"That's all I can break off," said Noah, panting. More daylight showed, but the hole still wasn't big enough for a person to fit through.

When Christianne moved back, her foot hit against something. She aimed her light at the floor. "I have an idea," she said, picking up the small shovel that had fallen out of the box when Nick dropped it. "Try the shovel, Noah."

She handed it to Nick who passed it up to Noah. He wedged it between a rafter and the broken roof board above it. By pushing against the handle, he was able to lever the board off.

"Yay!" said Christianne. "It worked!"

It was sort of like peeling an orange. Once he got a section off, the boards next to it pried up quite easily. The sky showed through the person-sized opening.

"All right!" Mandy said. "Climb through to the roof, Noah, but be careful. It could be kind of rotten. Christianne, you're next."

Nick helped her onto the makeshift ladder and she clambered up to the hole, where Noah helped her through.

Mandy turned off her light and tucked it in her pocket. "Don't forget the box of stuff," she said to Nick. She started up the bed frame, testing each spot before she put her full weight on it.

"Hey," said Nick. "Why am I always last?"

Mandy grinned down at him. "Well, you did say you weren't going to stand on this thing. So good luck getting out."

"Grrr," he growled. He hefted the cardboard box and carefully started up the bedframe. But because he had to hold the box with two hands, he couldn't grab the frame or tree trunk to steady himself. The rusted metal spring under his left foot broke away.

"Yow!" yelled Nick.

He plummeted to the floor.

Chapter 12. Outlaws of the Old West

"So did you find any gold dust?" Blake asked.

At the camp store Nick plopped the cardboard box of equipment on the counter after Mandy had fished out the blue pan. "Uh, no, we didn't."

"It can take a few tries," said the young storekeeper, "but if you're persistent, you'll find some."

"Thanks for letting us use the gold-panning stuff," Mandy said. She stared at Nick to remind him not to say anything about the thief. "We really appreciate it."

"Any time," Blake replied, "since you took such good care of it." He winked and stowed the box under the counter. "Did you see Bigfoot out there?"

"We didn't see him, but we smelled him!" Christianne said. "He needs to take a bath!"

Blake chuckled and then his face became serious. He leaned closer to them over the counter. "Well, I've got to tell you something. There's an old Indian legend about Bigfoot."

"The Indians saw Bigfoot too?" Noah asked.

"Oh, yeah," Blake replied. "Bigfoot has been around a long time. They say if you're walking in the woods and you hear a stick being hit against a hollow log, beware, because that means you're in Sasquatch territory. Sometimes the sound is loud like he's using a big stick and sometimes it's sharper like he's got a small stick. Also, there have been rocks thrown in Bigfoot hotspots. So be careful out there."

"What's a hotspot?" asked Christianne.

Blake scratched his head. "Well, that's an area where there have been a lot of Bigfoot sightings. Like around here."

"Gee, uh, th-thanks, Blake," Nick said. "That's good to know."

After they were outside, Mandy glanced at the frightened faces of the younger kids. "I don't believe any of that. He's just trying to scare us."

"But why, Mandy?" Christianne asked. "Blake is our friend."

It was 4:00 in the afternoon when the children breezed into the camp and let the screen door close behind them with a bang.

"Ah, the troops are home," Uncle Ross said, glancing up from the fly he was tying.

"About time too," said Aunt Ariel. "Where have you kids been? I was getting worried. And why are your clothes wet? What have you been doing?"

Mandy sighed. Those were hard questions to answer. Before Nick could bumble out a reply, she jumped in. Keep it simple, she thought. "We were panning for gold in the stream and when we got done, we decided to take a swim."

It was the truth, just the shortened version. At the old cabin in the woods, Nick had gotten a few bumps and bruises falling off the bed frame. In a grumpy mood, he had refilled the gold-panning box and held it up over his head, making Mandy hang over the edge of the hole to grab it. Then he scaled the bed frame like a big monkey, grasping the tree trunk for dear life.

They were all so dirty, when they got to the stream they jumped in with their clothes on and washed off as much grime as they could. They made sure to take turns guarding the box so it didn't disappear again.

"Did you have any luck?" Uncle Ross asked.

Nick shook his head. "No, Dad. But we learned how to do the panning from a video at the camp store and the guy there lent us some equipment. He said if we keep trying, we'll find some gold."

Mandy raised her eyebrows at him, reminding him not to say anymore about it. Changing the subject, she said, "I found a great keychain at the store for my collection." She took off her backpack to show them. "It's a miniature compass. The guy who works at the store said it's their best-seller."

"Well, it could come in handy sooner than you think," said Uncle Ross. "We have a surprise for all of you. We heard there's a geocache hidden in the area, so tomorrow we're all going to look for it with GPS."

"What's geo-cash?" asked Christianne. "Is that money? Can we buy something with it?"

Her father smiled. "No, but it *is* a treasure of sorts. It's a container that has a logbook and random small items in it. We sign the book and then we can take something out, but we have to put something else in of equal or greater value."

"Goody!" Christianne exclaimed. "We're going treasure hunting!"

Noah's forehead wrinkled in thought. "Well, we're not getting something for free. We're trading. What kind of things do we put in it?"

Aunt Ariel turned from the stove where she was cooking spaghetti sauce. "I thought we'd go over to the camp store and pick up some little souvenir thingies – you know like bottle openers or refrigerator magnets."

"Oh, like mine?" Noah said, pulling his Bigfoot bottle opener out of his pocket. "I bought it for Dad."

Uncle Ross chuckled. "Well, Bigfoot is certainly popular around here. It's a great tourist gimmick. Everyone hopes they'll see Bigfoot lurking in the woods, but if they really did, they'd be scared out of their gourd."

"That's for sure," Nick muttered, locking eyes with Mandy.

Mandy decided it would be best to avoid talking about Bigfoot too. "Uh, where do we get GPS, Uncle Ross?"

"Well, your Aunt Ariel and I have it on our phones," her uncle said. "We downloaded the app to join the geocache network. That will tell us the coordinates of the stash. Then we just follow the GPS to find it."

"That sounds like fun," Mandy said.

"When are we going?" asked Christianne. "I can't wait to see what's in the treasure box!"

"We thought it would be a nice morning activity," her mother replied. "We'll start out right after breakfast tomorrow."

That night the children settled into their bunk beds. Noah and Christianne played the 'What Object Am I Thinking Of?' guessing game while Nick read a book by flashlight. He had found *Outlaws of the Old West* on a shelf in the kitchen. Mandy had her light on too and was studying the drawing from the old prospector's tin box.

"Hey!" Mandy said. "The cabin the old prospector drew could be the one we found today! It looked really old."

Nick lowered his book. "I still can't figure out why someone would trap us inside the cabin."

"We were getting too close to something, that's why," Mandy replied. "Something they didn't want us to find."

Christianne and Noah stopped their game to listen.

"Maybe it *is* a treasure map!" said Christianne. "The thief doesn't want us to find the treasure."

"Because he's trying to find it first!" Noah added.

Mandy turned the drawing around. "So it shows what we think are the big hollow redwood tree, the stream, the cabin, a different kind of tree, and some cylinders. The old prospector lived in the first tree. The fact that he hid this drawing and the key shows he didn't want anyone else to see them."

"Why didn't he live in the cabin?" Noah asked.

"Maybe someone else was living there," guessed Nick. "Hey, guys, listen to this. This book says that a lot of the outlaws in northern California started out as prospectors in the Gold Rush. Some, like Black Bart and Rattlesnake Dick, gave up prospecting and started robbing stagecoaches that carried the gold. They made a lot more money that way."

"Stealing is wrong," Christianne said in a stern voice.

"Of course it's wrong," her brother said, "but these were bad guys. They didn't care. They wanted gold any way they could get it."

"Did they hurt people to get the gold?" asked Noah.

"Yeah, sometimes," Nick said. "This Mexican bandit, Joaquin (*Wah-keen'*) Murieta, was *really* bad. He and his gang attacked settlers and wagon trains and killed lots of people. The California Rangers tracked them down and, in a gun battle, Murieta was killed. The Rangers needed to prove he was dead to get their reward, so they cut off his head and preserved it in a big jar of alcohol."

"Nick, that's so gross!" Mandy exclaimed.

"Yup, just like Blackbeard the pirate," said Nick. "Remember him?"

How could Mandy forget seeing his head, a replica but very real-looking, in the Pirate and Treasure Museum in St. Augustine, Florida?

"Wow, here's another cool fact!" Nick continued. "The outlaws were always on the run and often buried their stolen gold, intending to go back and dig it up later. Just like pirates, they sometimes died and no one else knew where the treasure was buried. Supposedly, there's still a lot of gold out there that was never recovered!"

"Well, people do sometimes find those hidden treasures," said Noah. "Look what happened to my parents."

"Yeah, they hit the jackpot!" Nick agreed. "But it's not likely to happen to us. All we have is some old drawing that we don't understand."

"And a key!" Mandy added. "Don't forget the key. We just have to figure out what it opens." She stared at the drawing. "I hate to say this, but if this is the cabin we found today, we'll have to go back."

"Huh?" said Nick. "Are you kidding? That place is dangerous!"

"We'll be more careful next time," Mandy said. "Someone's trying to keep us away for a reason. I want to know why."

"Tell us more about the outlaws, Nick," said his sister.

Nick scanned the pages. "Well, this guy called Black Bart was kind of different. It says he was an English gentleman bandit and never shot anyone, even though he carried a shotgun. He robbed Wells Fargo stagecoaches in northern California 28 times between 1875 and 1883." Nick snorted. "He was scared of horses and did his robberies on foot. That's kind of wimpy. He wore a long black coat, a bowler hat and covered his head with a flour sack with holes cut out to see through."

"Is there a picture?" Noah asked, slipping out of the lower bunk and stepping up on the ladder to take a look.

"Yeah, there is," Nick replied. He turned the book toward Noah and held the flashlight on the page.

Noah studied the old brown-toned photo of a man with piercing eyes, a receding hairline, bushy white mustache and short beard. "He kind of looks like a Civil War general. My dad has a big book in his study with pictures like that."

"Actually, he fought in the Civil War," said Nick. "He was a good soldier and worked his way up to first lieutenant."

"Can I see?" asked Christianne, jumping out of bed.

Nick handed the open book to Noah, who passed it down to Christianne. She carried it to her bed and climbed up the other ladder so she and Mandy could both look at the picture.

"He looks like a nice grandfather," Christianne said.

Mandy flipped to a different page. "Well, he was married and had four kids but they lived far away in Illinois. They probably didn't even know he was a robber." She scanned the page with her flashlight. "Nick, did you see this? He's also called Black Bart the Poet. He used to leave a poem behind at the scene of the crime. Here's one of them.

'Here I lay me down to sleep
To wait the coming morrow,
Perhaps success, perhaps defeat,
And everlasting sorrow.
Let come what will, I'll try it on,
My condition can't be worse;
And if there's money in that box
'Tis munny in my purse.'

"Hey, wait a minute," said Mandy, setting down the book and picking up the drawing. "Doesn't that sound kind of familiar?" She stared at the back of the paper at the words written in faded ink and read them out loud.

"I labored long and hard for gold,
In many years of trying,
But when I took it brave and bold,
I left some others crying."

Mandy squinted at a couple of tiny squiggles that followed the poem. "It's signed BB."

"Wow," breathed Christianne. "BB must stand for Black Bart!"

"Awesome," said Noah. "So maybe the drawing wasn't made by the old prospector. Maybe it *is* a map and it belonged to an outlaw!"

Chapter 13. The Search

"All right, team, be ready to roll in five minutes!" said Uncle Ross the next morning. "We'll meet on the porch."

Aunt Ariel was packing a picnic lunch in a big gray backpack. "Be sure to wear your sneakers and put on some bug spray. The mosquitoes are as thirsty as little vampires this morning."

The four children rinsed their cereal bowls and stacked them in the sink. Then they headed to their room to don socks and sneakers and grab their jackets.

"This is going to be fun!" said Christianne, sticking her head through her pink hoodie. "Finally we get to find some treasure!"

"Don't get too excited," Nick said. "It will just be some cheap little thing like the stuff Mom bought."

Christianne glared at her brother. "It will still be fun."

"Don't be a 'spoil sport,' Nick," Mandy said, putting on her backpack. "It's all about the search, not what you end up with."

"Actually, I like the Bigfoot bottle opener a lot that I got for my father," said Noah. "I wouldn't mind having one of my own."

A shrill whistle sounded from outside.

"Uh, oh, we're late," said Nick. "We better move it."

On the porch, both Uncle Ross and Aunt Ariel had their phones out.

"So the stash is .8 of a mile away," said Uncle Ross. "That's not too far to walk. Although that's as 'the crow flies' so it could actually be farther."

"Shouldn't we bring a shovel?" asked Christianne. "To dig up the box?"

Her father shook his head. "The people who hide geocaches aren't allowed to bury them. I suppose it's to protect nature so searchers won't be digging holes all over the place. That could sure make a mess."

"So we'll be able to see it?" Noah asked.

"Probably not," said Aunt Ariel. "Some are very tricky to find and they're for experienced geocachers. All of them are hidden in some way. It might be disguised to look like a rock or a log or might be covered by a clump of ferns."

"The stash we're looking for," added Uncle Ross, "is called Tommy Turtle, it's medium-sized, and has a difficulty level of 1. That's the easiest to find. You can see all this on the screen."

He passed his phone to Nick and the other kids gathered round to take a look.

"Dad, does the container look like a turtle?" Christianne asked. "How do we find it?"

"It could look like a turtle – I don't know. We have the coordinates of where it's located – its latitude and longitude. We just follow the arrow until we get close, then we have to start looking around."

Christianne scrunched up her face. "What's lattie-tube and lonjie-tube?"

Nick rolled his eyes. "Picture a round globe, Christianne. The numbers tell how far from the equator and how far from the prime meridian the place is. You'll learn about it in school. Every location on earth has a different set of numbers."

He locked eyes with Mandy for a moment and she gave him a 'thumbs up.' They both remembered how important latitude and longitude had been in their last adventure in Florida.

Aunt Ariel handed her phone to Mandy. "We'd like you kids to try to figure this out. You and Christianne can use my GPS and the boys will have the other one. We'll only help you if you get stuck."

"All *right*!" said Christianne. "What do we do first?"

"Just start walking," her father replied. "You'll know you're getting closer to the geocache if the distance on the screen decreases."

"We'll lead," said Nick, stepping off the porch. "Come on, Noah."

"No, *we'll* lead!" said Christianne. "Girls rule, boys drool!"

"Stop right now," their mother commanded. "You can take turns. Boys first, since Nick is the oldest."

"Not fair," Christianne murmured, crossing her arms.

Mandy nudged her. "Here, you can carry the phone. It's going to take all of us working together to find the geocache."

Nick and Noah followed the arrow, which led them past the camp store and across the clearing. Everyone else headed the same way.

"Great, now what do we do?" asked Nick. The arrow pointed to a thicket of prickly bushes that stretched several yards in both directions.

"Let's take this path over here," Mandy suggested. She had a map of the park trails. "It looks like it will take us the right way." She and Christianne took over the lead.

They all followed the path, which wound in and out among the tall redwoods. As usual, wisps of fog drifted through the forest, creating a mystical atmosphere.

"What a pretty little plant," Aunt Ariel said. She crouched down to take a photo of some low-growing heart-shaped leaves topped here and there with dainty pink flowers. "They look like shamrocks."

"It's called *oxalis oregana* or redwood sorrel," said Uncle Ross, referring to the park brochure. "Here's an interesting fact. It's very sensitive to the sunlight. When the sun shines directly on it, the leaves fold downward. When the shade returns, they open again. With all this fog, I imagine they're usually open." Uncle Ross rubbed his hand across the rough, reddish bark of a tree by the path. "These sequoias are amazing." He tipped his head back to look up through the branches. "You can't even see the tops."

Aunt Ariel nodded. "They've been growing a long time. It's even more amazing they survived over a 1000 years without being cut down."

The children were so excited about the search they soon left the lagging grown-ups behind.

Farther down the trail, the girls were still in the lead with the boys right behind them. Mandy suddenly froze. She raised her hand to stop the others and raised a finger to her lips. "Do you hear that?" she whispered.

The children listened. A clunking noise, like a big stick hitting a hollow log, sounded through the woods.

"Do you think that's Mom and Dad making tree music?" Christianne asked. She moved closer to Mandy.

"I don't think so," Nick said. "Remember the Indian legend Blake told us about?" He gulped. "We're in Sasquatch territory."

The four of them huddled together, peering in all directions. The mist seemed thicker, turning every object into a vague mysterious shape.

"Over there," Noah murmured, pointing at a huge tree trunk as wide as a car.

They all stared at the spot. A big dark figure glided across an opening between that tree and the next. It disappeared into the murkiness.

As they stood with their mouths open, a round rock the size of a fist thudded onto the path just ahead of them.

"Oh no," squeaked Christianne. "Bigfoot is back."

"And he's not happy we're here," added Noah.

Chapter 14. Too Many Clues

The four children stood on the path without moving, their GPS arrows pointing to the spot where they had last seen the mysterious figure.

"L-Let's wait for Mom and Dad to catch up," Christianne said in a shaky voice. "What's taking them so long?"

Finally, they heard the murmur of voices and the grownups rounded a bend in the trail.

"Sorry, guys," said Uncle Ross. "We got a little distracted. There's a lot to see here.'"

"Uh, Dad, did you hear a weird sound a few minutes ago?" Nick asked.

His father shook his head. "No, these woods are really peaceful. Why do you ask?"

Mandy gave Nick a warning look. *Don't mention Bigfoot*, she pleaded, using mental telepathy.

"Oh, nothing," Nick said, getting the message. "We thought we heard something. Anyway, we don't know which way to go now. The GPS is pointing where there's no path."

His father consulted the park brochure with its map of trails. "Well, it looks like we have no choice but to continue this way. The path meanders back and forth, but basically heads southwest toward the geocache."

Mandy slid off her backpack and checked the little compass on its keychain. She lined up the arrow with the north mark. "You're right, Uncle Ross. The compass says we're going southwest."

"Good for you, Mandy!" said Aunt Ariel. "Nick, check the distance on the GPS. We started at .8 of a mile. What is it now?"

Nick studied the phone screen. "It says .5. That's a half a mile. We still have a long way to go."

"Be patient," said his father. "It's all about the journey."

"Who's turn is it to lead?" asked his mother.

"Your turn, Nick," said Mandy. She had no desire to be hit by a rock thrown by an angry ape man.

He raised an eyebrow at her. "That's okay, you can go ahead."

"Big chicken," Mandy muttered under her breath, and then said in a normal voice, "Come on, Christianne.'"

"Uh, I think I'll walk with Mom." The little girl grabbed her mother's hand.

Mandy didn't blame her one bit. She wouldn't mind holding someone's hand herself, but she didn't want to look like a wimp. She noticed that Noah had sneaked his hand into Uncle Ross's. She took a deep breath and started walking up the path, one

nervous step after another. Her eyes moved in a constant triangle from the arrow on the GPS to the misty woods on one side and then the other. She hoped she could duck in time if another rock hurtled out of the trees.

"Hey!" Nick hissed in her ear, making her jump. "Speed it up a little. At this rate, it will be Christmas before we get there."

Mandy whirled around and glared at him. "Any time you want to take over, feel free. Are you hiding behind me?"

"Of course not," he said. "I'm not afraid."

She crossed her arms. "Yeah, right."

"Really," he insisted. Nick stepped up beside her. "No reason why we can't do this together. The path is wide enough."

After awhile they came to a clearing. In the middle towered the second largest tree Mandy had ever seen. She stopped to read the sign beside it. "Colonel Jackson, 300 feet tall, 14 feet in diameter, 1350 years old," she read. "Wow," she breathed. "It's almost as big as the Old Prospector!"

"Yeah, cool," said Nick, craning his neck to look up. The wooden giant disappeared into the fog. He glanced around the clearing. "There are a couple of paths branching off from here. Which one should we take?"

"Let's look at the map again," Mandy suggested. She took it out of her pocket and unfolded it. "Here's the Colonel Jackson tree." She pointed at its name on the map. "Both of the paths start out in the right direction, but then this one veers off to the left more." She consulted the compass which now hung from her jacket zipper pull. Then she followed the route with her finger. "I think we take the other one. It more or less goes southwest."

"This is harder than I thought," Nick said. "Without a map and a compass, we'd be doing a lot of guessing."

"You kids are doing great," said Aunt Ariel. "How far are we from the geocache now?"

"It says .1 mile!" Mandy exclaimed. "We're almost there."

"All right," said Uncle Ross. "That's about 500 feet. When we get within 300 feet, stop watching the arrow and just make sure
the distance is decreasing."

Christianne let go of her mother's hand. "Can I carry the GPS now, Mandy?"

"Sure," Mandy replied, handing her the phone. Maybe Bigfoot – or whoever – was done tossing rocks for the moment. It seemed safer being with the grownups.

Nick glanced over at Noah. "Would you like a turn, Noah?"

The little boy smiled up at him, his blue eyes sparkling. "Yes, please."

Nick gave him the other GPS, but stayed close as they continued down the trail. "Look, the number is in feet now and it's going down," Nick said, pointing to the screen. "Good job."

"103, 102, 101, 100!" Christianne announced. "We're really close."

"Okay, guys," said Uncle Ross. "This is the hardest part. At this point, the GPS might not be accurate. So I'll take the phones now. You have to think like the person who hid the geocache. Look around for a good hiding place."

They all stopped to survey their surroundings. The path had led them to another clearing. A rustic bench made of split logs provided a good spot for the grownups to sit down.

Aunt Ariel waved a hand around the clearing. "Just ask yourself, where would you hide a container here so it wouldn't be too hard to find?" She switched on her camera so she could take pictures of their search.

The children spread out, peeking under ferns and behind trees. Many years ago, one of the giants of the forest had fallen. The top part of the tree had been cut away, leaving its enormous trunk. Its surface was green with moss, and ferns had taken root in the bark's crevices.

Christianne stared at the log through squinted eyes. "It looks like a huge turtle." Her eyes flew open. "A turtle! Tommy Turtle!"

Noah scurried to one end of the log. "It's hollow inside!" he exclaimed. He disappeared into the log.

"Wait for me!" Christianne called, racing after him.

Together they carried out a green-and-tan camo tackle box, like a fisherman would use. "We found it!" We found it!" they both said at once. They set it down on the bench.

Mandy and Nick crowded in behind them.

"Go ahead and open it," said Uncle Ross.

Christianne undid the latch and lifted the lid. "Awesome!" she said, clapping her hands. "Treasure!"

In each of the compartments that usually held fish hooks or lures nestled a small prize – a toy turtle, rubber ducky, bracelet, key chain.

The children took turns choosing an item and then Aunt Ariel filled in the spaces with souvenirs from the camp store. Under the tray, Uncle Ross found the logbook and jotted down the date and their names.

"I love this peace sign key ring!" said Mandy. "I can add it to my backpack collection. . . That's strange," she said, opening the small Ziploc bag. "There's a note in here too." She read it out loud.

"Open your eyes and you will see
What many have tried to find,
Go back to where the colonel's tree
Stands tall beside a sign."

"It's a clue," said Noah.

Christianne wrinkled her face. "A clue to what? We already found the treasure."

"Interesting," said Uncle Ross. "I've heard about a special kind of geocache called a mystery or puzzle cache, but I've never seen one before. The hider leaves clues that lead you from place to place."

"Oh," Nick said, "Kind of like what you did for my 10th birthday, Mom. Remember you wrote rhyming clues for my friends and me to find and they led us to a treasure chest filled with candy and prizes? That was the best party ever!"

Mandy studied her park map. "Well, it must mean the Colonel Jackson tree that we just passed. It's the only tree in the park that has 'colonel' in its name."

"Let's take a look on the way back," suggested Aunt Ariel.

"Yippee, let's go!" shouted Christianne.

The four children raced down the path, back to the previous clearing. They crowded close to the gigantic sequoia, studying every crack and crevice in its bark from eye level down.

Nick shrugged. "There's nothing here except a few bugs. Someone was just goofing off with that note."

"Wait!" Mandy said. "It mentions the sign. Let's check it out."

They stepped over to the informational sign and looked it over. Big yellow letters were painted on a brown board. The sign, topped with screw eyes, hung from a sturdy wooden framework.

"Here's something!" said Noah, crouching behind one of the posts. "It's taped to the wood."

The children crowded around him. Nick reached down and pried the duct tape from the post. The tape had been painted brown to blend in with the sign. Underneath it was a small plastic cylinder. Nick snapped off the lid and tapped the open end into his hand. A folded piece of paper dropped out. He handed it to Mandy.

"Another clue!" said Christianne. "Open it, Mandy!"

Mandy unfolded it and read:

"Not far from here there is a beast
Whose teeth are made of wood
To find the way just head northeast
It guards the place of goods"

They all frowned in thought, trying to make sense of the riddle.

"Does Bigfoot have wooden teeth?" asked Christianne.

Nick rolled his eyes. "No, silly, but George Washington did."

She squinted at him. "You're making that up. President Washington didn't have wooden teeth."

"He did so. I learned it in school."

"What are goods?" Noah asked. "Is that the opposite of bads?"

Mandy looked at him, thinking hard. "My guess is that goods are things they sell in a store. The nearest place like that is the camp store. She checked the park map. "That's the direction we're traveling in now – northeast."

"Hey!" said Nick. "The beast with the wooden teeth must be one of those chainsaw carvings by the store!"

Just then Uncle Ross and Aunt Ariel caught up with them. "What did you find?" Aunt Ariel asked.

"Another clue," Nick replied. "May we go on ahead to the camp store?"

"Sure," said his father, "but stay on the trail. We don't want you to get lost. We'll meet you at the camp."

"Come on, I'll race you!" Christianne shouted, and shot down the path like a pink bullet.

The other three children took off after her. Their run became a jog and then a fast walk, as they all slowed down to catch their breath. At last they arrived at the camp store.

"Uh, oh," said Noah. "There are *five* beasts and they *all* have wooden teeth!"

The children surveyed the chainsaw carvings in front of the store – a bear, a deer, a beaver, a wolf and a bighorn sheep.

"Well, only two of them have their mouths open," said Christianne, 'the wolf and the bear." She walked over to the wolf and stared between its sharp teeth. "Nothing here."

The bear, upright on its hind feet, was taller than all of them.

"We need something to stand on," Mandy said.

Nick grabbed a metal pail from the porch and turned it upside down beside the bear. He hopped up on it and peered into the snarling mouth. "Here it is!" He fished out a three-inch wide rolled up piece of paper.

"Let me see, let me see!" said his sister, trying to climb up on the bucket.

"Look out!" Nick yelled. He lost his balance and fell off the pail, landing on his bum. "Ouch." Slowly, he got to his feet, glaring at his sister.

"Sor-ree," Christianne said, shrugging. "I just wanted to see the clue."

Nick unrolled the paper and cleared his throat. He read it to the others.

"Along the river and through the woods
To the prospector's house you go.
You all know the way
To where he did stay
While hiding so long ago."

"Brother," Nick muttered. "That's shabby poetry. Sounds like a cross between 'Over the River' and 'Little Red Riding Hood.'"

Christianne wrinkled her nose. "I thought the prospector lived in the tree."

"Maybe a different prospector lived in the cabin," Noah suggested, "but why was he hiding?"

Mandy frowned. "We know about a prospector-turned-outlaw who had to hide. Black Bart. Maybe it's talking about him. You know what this means, don't you?"

"What?" the other three asked.

"We have to go back. There's something important at that cabin in the woods. . . and we need to find out what."

Chapter 15. Back to the Cabin

The next day the four children stood at the edge of the woods, peering between tree branches at the broken down cabin.

"I don't see why we had to come back here," Nick said in a low voice. "We're just asking for trouble."

"This is where the clue led us," Mandy reminded him. "There's something here for us to find."

Nick shook his head. "Who wrote the clues anyway? And put the first one in the geocache? In fact, how did they know we would be hunting for the geocache? This is too freaky."

Mandy shrugged. "I don't know. Maybe we'll find out when we look inside. Everyone has their flashlight this time, right?"

Christianne nodded and pulled out her light. "Ready!" she said.

Noah shook his head. "Mine's in there somewhere, broken."

"Sorry, Noah," Nick said. "Here, take mine." He dug the mini-light out of his pocket and handed it to Noah.

"Okay, follow me," said Mandy, heading across the clearing. At the door she stopped. "Hmm, that's strange. The door's open now. Someone pulled out the nails." She set down the hammer they had borrowed from Blake to pry the door open.

"Great," muttered Nick. "Come right in and let us trap you again." He refused to step through the opening. "You go ahead and look around. I'm going to stay right here and make sure no one sneaks up on us." He picked up the hammer to use as a weapon.

The other three snapped on their lights and stepped into the gloomy interior. Daylight showed through the hole in the roof.

"What are we looking for?" Christianne asked, shining her flashlight on the warning written in red. She shivered.

"I don't know," Mandy replied. "Anything we didn't notice last time, I guess. We didn't get to finish our search before the door got hammered shut." She aimed her light at the nearest wall and slowly panned it back and forth from top to bottom.

Christianne stayed close to Mandy. Noah started moving away from the girls, keeping his beam focused on the dirt floor of the cabin. The floor was littered with fallen boards, piles of dry leaves, and a few things they didn't notice last time -- a wooden chair
with its back broken off, a ratty mattress, and a few other odds and ends. The metal bed frame, their makeshift ladder, still stood
on end beneath the hole in the roof.

"Hey, I didn't see this last time," Noah said.

Mandy looked over.

His light was shining on a long, unpainted wooden box.

She and Christianne picked their way through the clutter. In the bright beam of their three lights combined, Mandy noticed hinges on one side of the box. She also noticed there was no dust on top of it. Hmm. That meant it hadn't been in the cabin for long, just like the green tarp. She still didn't want to be the one to open it. What if there was a rattlesnake curled up inside? Heh, heh, she'd let Nick open it. But there was no way she was going to carry it to the door. Besides, it was too heavy.

"Nick," she yelled. "We found a box. Come see!"

Nick stuck his head inside the doorway. "One of you will have to change places with me. I'm not leaving this entrance unguarded!"

"Not me!" said Christianne. "I want to see what's in the box."

"Me too," Noah said. "I'm the one who found it," he reminded them.

Mandy was probably the most curious of all. What if was a treasure? But Nick was right. They had to stay alert. Whoever trapped them before could be watching them this very moment and be waiting for the chance to do something worse to them. She sighed. "I'll go." She made her way to the door. "Be careful opening the box, Nick. No telling what's inside."

Nick joined the younger kids at the box. "Did you open it yet?" he asked them.

They solemnly shook their heads.

"Nope," said Christianne. "If there's something bad in there, it will get you instead of us."

"Gee, thanks," her brother mumbled. He laid his hand on the lid and took a deep breath. Slowly he raised the cover. When the others shined their lights on what was inside, he almost had a heart attack.

"Ahhh!" screamed Christianne and Noah.

"What is it?" Mandy yelled from the doorway. "What did you find?"

Nick slammed the lid down and stood still for a moment, waiting for his heart to stop galloping. "Come take a look," he said.

"After hearing you all scream, I don't think I want to see it," Mandy said. "What is it?"

"Christianne, go guard the door," Nick told his sister. When the girls had changed places, he opened the box again.

The face of Bigfoot stared up at Mandy. Underneath it was a mound of reddish-brown fur. "A costume. Someone has been dressing up like Bigfoot!" Her eyes narrowed. "Someone's been playing tricks on us."

Noah touched the ape man's nose. "It sure looks real."

"So there's no Bigfoot?" asked Christianne from the doorway. "It's just fake?"

"Looks that way," Mandy replied. "I was right after all."

"Who would do this?" Nick asked, shaking his head.

"That's a really good question," said Mandy, thinking hard. "Blake's the one who's been telling us all about Bigfoot. Do you think it's him?"

Christianne crossed her arms. "No. Blake wouldn't do that. He's our friend."

"You said that before," her brother said. "But we don't really know him very well. He could have done it. He knew when we were going gold-panning and geocaching."

Noah shook his head. "He wouldn't steal his own gold-panning equipment, would he? That doesn't make sense."

"Someone wanted us to look in the cabin," Mandy reasoned. "I guess Blake wouldn't have wanted us to find the Bigfoot suit if he was the one who wore it. But he might be the one who led us here with the clues."

"Yeah," Nick agreed. "Remember, he noticed the keychain collection on your backpack, Mandy? He would have known you would go for the peace sign keychain in the geocache, so he planted it there with the poem!"

Mandy frowned. "I hate being so predictable. Anyway, let's assume for a moment that Blake wrote the poems. Why did he lead us here to find the box? Why wouldn't he just tell us someone is fooling around and pretending to be Bigfoot?"

"Maybe he didn't know the box was here," said Noah. "Maybe he wanted us to find something else.

"You might be right, Noah," Mandy said. "We should keep looking. Let's leave the box just like it is so whoever put it there won't know we found it. Then let's search this place from top to bottom. I have a feeling there's something else we're meant to find -- something more important than a monkey suit."

Chapter 16. Discovery!

"I'll go back to standing guard," said Nick. "You three go ahead and search the cabin." He changed places with his sister. "Okay," Mandy said to the younger children. "Look for anything unusual. Let's check every inch of the floor and walls."

"Could something be buried *under* the floor?" Christianne asked, shining her light on the hard-packed earth.

"It could," Mandy replied. "But I sure hope not. It would take us forever to dig up all of this."

Bit by bit, they studied each section of the interior. It was obvious the place hadn't been lived in for a *long* time. In addition to the hole in the roof, the owl roosting in the rafters and the broken-up furniture, the smell of decay clung to the cabin. It made Mandy's nose twitch. She tried to take shallow breaths. Questions rolled through her brain like ocean waves. Who had led them there and why? What were they supposed to find? And where was it?

Mandy shined her light on the warning on the wall. She shuddered. That was really scary. Who had written it? Obviously, someone *didn't* want them there. She scanned the wall above the message. Whoa, what was that? In the triangle where the two sides of the roof joined, another owl roosted. She started to duck, expecting it to zoom down at them like the first owl had, but it didn't move. *It's a carving*, she realized. Someone had hewn the shape of an owl from a piece of wood and mounted it in the space near the ceiling.

"Hey, guys, look at that," she said, keeping her light pointed at the owl.

Christianne and Noah looked up.

"An owl!" Christianne said. "I'm sure glad that one isn't alive."

Noah peered at it with his eyes scrunched. "Mandy, is there some way we can get up there to look at it better? I have an idea."

Mandy looked around. "Well, we can try the bed frame again. It worked as a ladder last time." She skirted the scattered junk to get to the post where the metal frame was still tied up on end. Her light reflected on something red on the floor. "Hey, it's your flashlight, Noah." She picked it up and flicked the switch, but nothing happened. "It must have broken when Nick fell." She handed it to the boy. "Oh, well, at least Nick gave you his. Shine it here for me," she said.

Christianne and Noah both focused their lights on Mandy's hands as she loosened the knots in the paracord. The three of them dragged the bed frame to the wall where the owl perched above.

"I don't know," said Mandy. "I don't want you to get hurt on this. There's nothing to tie the frame to over here."

"Maybe you and Nick could hold it while I climb up," Noah suggested. "You two are the strongest. No offense, Christianne."

The little girl sighed. "I suppose that means *I'll* have to be the lookout again. Don't you dare find treasure without me!"

"We won't," promised Mandy. "We'll just take a look at the owl."

Christianne made her way to the entrance and told Nick the plan.

He handed her the hammer. "Don't let anybody near this door."

She wrinkled her nose. "If someone comes, do I hit them with the hammer?"

He snorted. "Yeah, right. You might be able to overpower an ant. If it's anything else, just yell and we'll come running. Give me your light."

She glared at him and handed him the little blue flashlight. "Don't break it like you did Noah's!" She turned to face the woods, holding the hammer in front of her with both hands.

Nick snapped on the light and shuffled over to where Mandy and Noah waited. "So you found an owl? Where is it?"

Noah aimed his flashlight up at the owl carving. "If you and Mandy will hold the bed frame, I want to climb up and look at that. I think I can just reach it. It seems strange that owls keep popping up around here. Mom read me a story once about an owl that brought a message to an Indian boy from his grandfather who had died. Maybe that owl has something to tell us."

Nick raised one eyebrow. "Okay, if you say so." He steadied one side of the frame, while Mandy grasped the other side.

"How can I hold the light and climb too?" Noah wondered out loud. "Wait, I've got an idea!" He found a roll of duct tape in one of the pockets of his camper shorts. Using the scissors on his jackknife, he cut off a six-inch piece of tape. He removed his baseball cap and taped the little flashlight to the visor. After stowing his equipment back in their compartments, he turned on the light and set the hat back on his head. "There, now I have a headlamp."

Mandy grinned at him. "You're amazing."

He smiled back. "Hold on. . . here I go."

Noah clambered up the metal 'ladder' as high as he could. Then he examined the carving with one hand while bracing himself against the wall with the other. Up close he could see all the whittle marks made by the knife that carved the wood. He studied each part of the owl. "That's funny," he said. "The beak looks like it was made from a separate piece of wood and added on. There's a crack all around it."

"See if you can move it," Mandy suggested.

He grabbed the beak and wiggled it. It pivoted to the side. Noah dipped his head a little so the light beam zeroed in on the beak. "All *right*!" he said. "There's a key hole!"

Mandy's eyes widened. "A keyhole?" She stared at Nick.

"And we have a key," he said, "don't we?"

"We sure do. It's in my backpack. . . Don't move, Noah. I have to let go for a minute."

Mandy pushed against the bed frame with her hip and struggled out of her pack. She unzipped a pocket and fished out the tin box from the Old Prospector. She pried off the cover and took out the key. "Here, Noah, try it and see if it fits." She passed it up to him.

Noah pushed the key into the slot and tried turning it. It wouldn't budge. "It doesn't work," he said in frustration.

"Don't give up yet," Nick said. "Keys can be tricky. Try jiggling it or pulling it out a little bit. The lock could be rusty."

"Did you find something?" Christianne called, taking a step inside.

"We'll let you know if we do, Christianne," Nick said impatiently. "Don't you dare leave that door unguarded!"

Noah tried again. He jiggled and wiggled, pulled and pushed. When he pushed, the key slid in a little farther. He turned it to the right and heard a faint click. "It fit, it fit!" he said. "But how do I open it?"

"Try pushing on something!" Mandy said. "An eye, an ear."

Noah tried pushing on both eyes and both ears of the owl but nothing happened. Then he pressed on the beak. "Whoa!" he shouted, as the whole owl sprang open. He grasped the wall to keep his balance.

From below, Mandy and Nick watched with excitement.

"What is it?" Nick asked. "What's in there?"

"There's a hollow space inside," said Noah. "Like a little triangle-shaped cupboard." He reached in and pulled something out. "There's a book."

"A book?" Nick said in a disappointed voice. "Why would anybody lock up a book?" He looked over his shoulder and called to his sister. "Christianne, we found a book—nothing to get excited about."

There was no reply.

"Does it say anything on the cover, Noah?" Mandy asked.

Noah wiped the small book on his shirt to free it of dust. "Nope." Then he opened it. "But inside there's a name."

"Can you read it?" asked Mandy.

"It looks like Charles Earl Bowles," said Noah. "And there's a year – 1875."

Mandy locked eyes with Nick.

"Black Bart!" he said. "It must be the outlaw's book!"

"Wow!" exclaimed Mandy. "Let's take a look!"

Noah stashed the book and key in his pocket and carefully climbed down the metal. It protested with loud squeaks. Just as his feet hit the floor, a scream ripped through the cabin.

Chapter 17. Attack!

"Help!" yelled Christianne, jumping through the doorway of the cabin. "Bigfoot is throwing rocks again!"

A sharp 'thunk' thudded against the outside wall.

"It isn't Bigfoot. He's a fake, remember?" Mandy said, hurrying over to the entrance. She pulled Christianne to the side. Then, with her body protected by the inner wall, she took a quick peek outside.

The bright sunlight dazzled her eyes. She couldn't see much of anything for a moment. She ducked back as a rock about the size of a baseball sailed through the doorway and landed on the dirt floor.

The boys scrambled to the wall as well.

"Whoever it is, he's crazy!" Nick said. "Someone could get a concussion!"

Rocks continued to rain against the outer wall.

"What are we going to do?" Christianne asked, her eyes wide with fear.

"We need to get out of here," Mandy said. "We're sitting ducks."

Nick groaned. "Don't make me climb up to the roof again. That bed frame is more dangerous than rocks – I could get impaled by a runaway spring!"

Noah grabbed the hammer and thrust it into Nick's hands. "Here, Nick. Maybe you can pry some boards off the back wall and make a hole big enough for us to crawl through."

"Good idea, Noah!" said Mandy. "I'll distract the guy while you work at that. Be as quiet as you can so he won't know what we're doing." She stuck her head out the doorway and then pulled it back in.

Another rock hit the wall.

"Christianne, see if you can find anything we can throw at *him*. But stay away from the entrance."

"Okay." The little girl snapped on her light again and scoured the floor alongside the side wall. She picked up a couple of broken boards and some rusty pieces of metal.

Staying in the shadows, Mandy made a lunge for the rock on the floor. She grabbed it and scuffled back to her protected spot. Taking a deep breath, she whirled toward the door, lifted her arm, hurled the rock as far as she could and then side-stepped to safety.

She heard a grunt in the bushes. "Yes!" she said in a low voice, pumping her fist in victory. "That will show him."

"You throw really good," Christianne said, as she hauled her finds over to her cousin.

"I play Little League at home," Mandy explained. "But I think that was a lucky shot. I wish we had more rocks, but that's the only one that came into the cabin.. . . Let's see what you've got." She examined the possible ammunition. "Well, I don't think the boards would go far, but the iron pieces should work. I'll save them in case the guy gets closer to the door."

No more rocks were thrown for awhile.

"Good, maybe he's gone," Mandy murmured to Christianne. She peered around the doorframe.

Another rock clunked against the cabin right next to her. Mandy actually felt the breeze of it against her face. "Shoot," she said. "No such luck."

The screech of releasing nails came from the back corner of the cabin as Nick levered off a board. A bright slash of daylight gleamed through the hole. Once he had the first one off, two more came away easily.

"One more ought to do it," Noah encouraged. He could already fit through the opening, but the bigger kids would need more space.

"Almost ready," Nick called to Mandy. "Send Christianne over." He pried off another board. "Okay, go on out," he said to Noah.

Noah slithered through the hole and Christianne followed him.

"Throw something and then run," Nick told Mandy. He crouched down and started through the opening. He was halfway through when one of his belt loops caught on a sliver of wood. "Help!" he cried. "I'm stuck!"

Christianne and Noah each took one of his hands and pulled.

Meanwhile, Mandy heaved one of the iron pieces through the doorway and then scurried to the back corner. "Hurry up, Nick!" she urged, pushing on his feet.

"Cut it out, Mandy!" Nick wheezed. "I can't move. My pants are caught on something."

"Good grief, Nick," she said. "You need to cut down on the potato chips!"

She felt around the opening and found where the belt loop curled around a sharp piece of wood. She picked up the hammer and pushed at the thick splinter until it broke off. The little kids were still tugging on his hands. All of a sudden Nick flew through the hole like a cork popping out of a bottle.

"Ouch," he said, lying full-length on the ground.

Mandy scrambled through the hole and over Nick.

"Ow, ow, ow," he said into the dirt.

"Get up, Nick, we have to go!" Mandy said.

Nick raised his head and glared at her. "Do you think I'm a bearskin rug or something?" He struggled to his feet. "Which way do we go?"

"I don't know," said Mandy, panic in her voice. "Just away from here! In a few minutes, he'll get suspicious and look in the cabin."

Nick pushed through the thick shrubbery with the other three close behind him. Branches scratched their arms and faces.

"Do you think we should hide in the bushes until he goes away?" Nick whispered.

"What if he *doesn't* go away?" Mandy retorted. "For some reason this guy is out to get us. He's *not* going to give up!"

"I'm scared," said Christianne, her face puckered up like she was ready to cry.

"Don't worry," Mandy whispered, taking her hand. "He's not going to catch us. Come on." Praying she didn't step on a snake, Mandy pushed past Nick. With Christianne in tow and with Noah right behind them, Mandy led them through the forest.

After awhile, they began seeing redwood trees and the undergrowth thinned out. It was much easier going, but Mandy felt more exposed. She wished they could just sit down for a moment and rest. The little kids' feet were dragging. Now that the adrenaline rush had died down, she felt tired too. But there was no safe place to stop. Bright sunlight filtered through the branches of the tall trees instead of the usual mist.

"Mandy, look at that!" Christianne said, pointing to a dark space at the base of a redwood giant.

The children stumbled over to the tree.

Clicking on her light, Mandy crouched down and peered inside. The hollow base of the tree looked like a troll cave, dark and rooty, not as big as the space inside the Old Prospector, but big enough. Some dry leaves had drifted inside and lay like a carpet on the floor. Mandy found a long stick and poked at the leaves, making sure nothing slithery lay underneath them.

"Okay, guys, this looks like a good place to hide for a few minutes and rest," she said. She scrambled into the hole.

The other three children followed Mandy into the black pit.

Chapter 18. A Voice From the Past

"While we're sitting here, let's take a look at the outlaw's book," said Mandy in a low voice. Her curiosity was like an itch that needed to be scratched.

Noah took it out of his pocket and handed it to her. He also returned the key.

Mandy stashed the key in the tin box in her pack. Then she opened the front cover of the book and studied the signature. "Wow," she breathed. "Just imagine – Black Bart wrote this!"

Nick craned his neck to take a look. "Hey, maybe it's his diary. He might have kept track of all his robberies!"

Mandy turned a few pages. "No. It looks like a book of poems." She read in a whisper:

> *'So here I've stood while wind and rain*
> *Have set the trees a-sobbin'*
> *And risked my life for that fool stage*
> *That wasn't worth the robbin'.'*

"He must have left that after one of his robberies," said Noah. "I guess there wasn't much to steal that time."

As Mandy ruffled through the pages, a folded piece of paper dropped out. Christianne picked it up and opened it. "It's a letter."

"Let me see," said her brother, taking it from her. "Shine your light on it for me."

My dearest Mary,

"Oh, yuck, a love letter," Nick said.
"Wait," said Mandy. "Wasn't that the name of his wife in *Outlaws of the Old West*?" He must have written her a letter and never got to send it. Keep reading, but use a soft voice. We're hiding, remember?"

My dearest Mary,

How I wish I could see you again, but alas, that cannot be. I have made some poor choices in my life in the pursuit of riches. You would not want to look upon the man I have become – a thief and a robber. Though I am finished with all that now, my reputation is ruined, and I am no fit husband for you.

I think of you and the children often. I hope you received the money I sent and it was a help. I would send more, but it is not honest money and besides, there is no way to get it to you.

I write this from my heart, but realize you will never read these words. It is better you think I died working the hard life of a prospector.

With all my love,
Charlie

"That's sad," Christianne said. "He never got to see his kids again."

"Yeah," agreed her brother, "too bad. They might have thought it was cool to have an outlaw for a father!"

Christianne frowned. "His wife wouldn't want to be married to an outlaw."

Noah frowned at her. "I'm still wondering why his book of poems was locked up in the owl cupboard. Doesn't that mean he didn't want anyone to see it?"

Nick snickered. "Maybe he was embarrassed to have anyone read his lame poems."

"People *did* read them," said Mandy, "every time he left one after a robbery. There must be a better reason."

"He hid the book because," said Christianne, thinking hard, "because it must have something else in it. . . maybe a secret?"

"Hmm," Mandy said, riffling through the pages again. "Good idea, Christianne."
She turned to the last page that had writing on it. "This poem looks interesting. Listen to this.

"*Ten strides is all from door to tree*
Beside the kitchen midden
Remove the rock and strike with spade
To find what has been hidden"

"That doesn't seem to have anything to do with a robbery," Nick said.

"What's a midden?" Noah asked. "I've never heard that word before."

"I have," said Nick. "For awhile I was really into learning about castles. I had this book that labeled all the parts – the ramparts, the moat, the courtyard – and one area was the kitchen midden where they threw away garbage. It was the castle dump."

"In the old days, probably every house and cabin had a place like that," said Mandy. "There weren't any garbage trucks back then."

"Did he hide something in a dump?" Christianne asked, puzzled. "Ick."

"Think about it," Mandy urged, her eyes shining with excitement. "Whoever lived in that old cabin in the woods had to throw their trash somewhere nearby. It sounds like maybe Black Bart hid something there. . . something he didn't want anyone to find, something besides his book of poems. In the letter, he says he has money, but can't get it to his family. Maybe *that's* what he hid!"

"His loot?" asked Nick. "From the robberies?"

Christianne and Noah glanced at each other. "Treasure!" they both shouted at once.

"We just have to find the dump," Mandy said, "and the treasure is ours! The poem gives us directions."

Nick moaned. "Oh, crud. That means we have to go back to that place *again*? Someone is out to get us, someone who belongs in the loony bin. We've been trapped and attacked. Who knows what they'll do next time?"

"But, Nick," argued Mandy, "we're the only ones with the clue. There's a treasure out there waiting for us. We *have* to go!"

"No, Mandy," said Nick, "it's just too dangerous. I absolutely, positively refuse to go there." He crossed his arms. "If any of you got hurt, Mom and Dad would disown me forever *after* they chop me up into little pieces and feed me to the bears."

"You're right, Nick," Mandy said.

"I am?" he asked, confused. Mandy hardly ever agreed with him.

"Yes, it *is* risky. We've got the Bigfoot imposter to watch out for. He seems to know something valuable is near that cabin and he doesn't want us finding it before he does. So we've got to trick him somehow so we can get to the dump safely. Any ideas?"

"Yeah, let's go back to camp and eat," Nick suggested. "I'm hungry."

"Okay," said Mandy. "Maybe food will help our brains think of an answer. We've *got* to figure this out. Black Bart's loot could be worth thousands of dollars!"

"Maybe millions!" said Noah.

"Maybe zillions!" said Christianne.

"Right now I'd settle for a cheeseburger," muttered Nick.

Chapter 19. Crime Doesn't Pay

"So what have you kids been up to today?" asked Uncle Ross.

Everyone was seated at the picnic table outside the camp, enjoying potato salad, corn on the cob, and Nick's favorite--cheeseburgers. For a moment, no one said anything in reply, as the children all thought about how to answer that question without alarming the grown-ups.

Finally, Mandy spoke up. "Um, we did more exploring. There's a lot to see in this campground."

Aunt Ariel set a bowl of fresh strawberries on the table. "Did you find anything interesting?"

"Actually, we did," said Mandy. A sudden flash of inspiration had given her a brilliant idea. "We found another clue -- one of those poems."

"How many is that now?" Uncle Ross asked.

"Number 4," Mandy replied. "I think this is going to lead us to the best geocache ever, but we need your help."

The other children stared at Mandy. Was she going to tell all? Would the grown-ups even believe them? Or worse yet, would the kids get in trouble?

Mandy cleared her throat. "Well, we think the clue says we have to dig to find the cache. I know usually that isn't allowed, so we hope you'll go with us to see if it's okay. It's in kind of an old dump in the woods."

Uncle Ross and Aunt Ariel looked at each other, both with eyebrows raised.

"Sounds interesting," said Uncle Ross. "We'll see if we can scare up a shovel. I've always been intrigued by these puzzle geocaches."

"We'll head out right after breakfast tomorrow morning," said Aunt Ariel. "Thanks for including us in your adventure. It should be fun."

As the children got ready for bed that night, Nick turned to Mandy with a frown on his face. "That was clever making Mom and Dad think we're searching for a geocache. But they're going to find out we went in the old cabin. How do we explain that without getting into trouble?"

"We'll think of something," Mandy said. "I don't know what yet."

"At least the bad guy won't attack us with Mom and Dad there," said Christianne. "Will he?"

Noah shook his head. "People don't always believe kids, but they believe grown-ups. He could get arrested if he tried anything."

"I agree with Noah," said Mandy. "That's what I'm counting on anyway." She climbed the ladder to the top bunk and slipped into her sleeping bag. "So, Nick, do you still have that book, *The Outlaws of the Old West*?"

"Sure do," Nick said, sliding it from underneath his pillow. "What do you want to know?"

"Does it list Black Bart's robberies? If so, when was the very last one?"

Nick opened the book to the end of the chapter about Charles Bowles. "The first one was on July 26, 1875 and the last one was on June 23,

1883. That's funny. He robbed the same stagecoach both times. It traveled from Sonora to Milton in Calaveras County. The first time he got away with it, but the last time he was shot in the hand. He escaped but left some things behind – drops of blood on the ground, food, eyeglasses, and a handkerchief marked with F. X. O. 7. Two Wells Fargo detectives contacted every laundry in San Francisco – there were 90 of them -- until they found the one that used that mark. Black Bart was tracked down at a boardinghouse in San Francisco. He told them his name was T.Z. Spalding, but they found a Bible in his room, a gift from his wife, and his real name, Charles E. Bowles, was written in it. He was arrested and sent to San Quentin Prison for four years."

"That was good detective work," said Noah, "finding someone from a handkerchief. It shows you that 'crime doesn't pay.' The bad guys always get caught in the end."

"There's more," said Nick. "When he got out of prison, he wasn't in very good shape – old, bad eyes, bad hearing. He told reporters he was done with a life of crime. He wanted to get away from everybody. Black Bart just kind of disappeared after that."

"*We* know where he went," said Mandy. "Here. He must have lived in that old cabin until he died."

"I bet he was really lonely," Christianne said. "No friends, no family, no dog."

Her brother snorted. "How do you know he didn't have a dog?"

She thought for a moment and then smiled. "I *don't* know. Maybe he *did* have a dog. I hope he had a dog. Then he wouldn't be so lonely."

Nick rolled his eyes. "Whatever. . . so what do we tell Mom and Dad about Black Bart's book? You know it probably belongs in a museum. It's a piece of history."

Mandy fluffed her pillow and sat up straighter. "We'll tell them the truth."

"*What*?" Nick squawked. "I'll be grounded for life!"

"Well, we don't need to mention being trapped and attacked," Mandy said, "just that the door to the cabin was open and we were curious, so we peeked in."

"The clues did lead us there," said Christianne. "We *had* to go in."

"And we saw the owl fly out," added Noah. "When we looked up at the ceiling, we found the owl cupboard and Black Bart's book was inside!"

"What about the Bigfoot costume?" Christianne asked. "Should we tell them about that?"

"Uh, no, I don't think so," said Mandy. "That would lead to a whole bunch of questions. Let's keep it simple."

Nick groaned. "Keep it simple? It's too complicated to keep it simple. We still don't know who wrote the clues, who pretended to be Bigfoot or who threw rocks at the cabin."

Mandy rested her chin in her hand, thinking hard. "It might not be the same person."

Nick groaned again. "You mean there might be more than *one* crazy person running around? Great. That makes it even *more* complicated!"

"Let's just concentrate on finding Black Bart's stash," Mandy suggested. "That's the important thing."

"If there *is* a stash," Nick muttered. "He could have spent it all on beans and bacon and comic books."

"Lights out, kids!" came a shout from the living room.

Noah jumped out of bed to click off the overhead light and then scurried back under the covers.

Darkness settled over them like a warm blanket. An owl hooted in the distance, out on its nightly mission to find a tasty meal.

Or maybe it's delivering a message to someone, Mandy thought. Everyone except her had drifted off to sleep.

She lay listening to the night sounds with questions ricocheting in her brain. Would they find Black Bart's loot the next day or was it long gone? Who was behind all the strange happenings? Would the kids be safe having Aunt Ariel and Uncle Ross with them or were they leading *them* into danger too?

Chapter 20. There's Gold in Them Thar Hills

"So tell us about the clues you've found so far," Aunt Ariel said the next morning.

Everyone had eaten, put on jackets and sneakers, and had gathered on the front porch. Uncle Ross held a shovel he had borrowed from another camper.

Mandy opened her backpack and took out three slips of paper. "Well, you were with us when we found the first poem in the geocache that led us to the Colonel Jackson tree."

"Taped behind the tree's sign was the second clue," Noah continued. "That took us to the carved bear in front of the camp store."

Christianne eagerly jumped in. "And that poem led us to a cabin in the woods. . . oops." Her face grew red. "I wasn't supposed to say that."

"It's okay, Christianne," Mandy reassured her. "That's where we're going now."

Uncle Ross frowned. "A cabin? Does someone live there? I hope you haven't been trespassing."

"It's deserted," said Mandy.

"And falling down," Nick added over his shoulder. He was leading the way. "No one has lived there for a long time."

As they followed the trail through the redwood forest, scarves of mist floated between the trees, turning it into a land of ghouls and goblins. Every tree trunk loomed like a threatening ogre.

Mandy shivered. Why couldn't the sun be shining? She felt cold between her shoulder blades as if x-ray eyes were drilling into her back. Was the attacker out there watching them? She noticed Noah glancing around. Did he feel it too?

When the path meandered out of the redwoods to the bank of the stream, the mist got thinner. The water glistened and foamed as it glided around the rocks.

"This is where we panned for gold," Nick explained. "Too bad we didn't find any."

"I imagine it takes more than one try," said his father. "You'd need a lot of time and patience. I've heard of people looking for years and never finding anything."

Christianne put her hands on her hips. "Blake says if you keep trying, you *will* find some gold dust."

Her father raised an eyebrow. "Who's Blake?"

"Oh, that's the nice young man at the camp store," said Aunt Ariel. "He's the owners' nephew. He helped us pick out some trinkets for the geocache."

Uncle Ross winked at Christianne. "Well, Blake ought to know. So where's this cabin?"

"Just a little farther," Nick said, leading them on. He rubbed his hands on the sides of his jeans in a nervous gesture. In awhile, he turned off the main trail onto the faint path the children had made through the long grass. "Here it is."

The graying, decaying cabin crouched in the brush like a big, hairy rat. It gave Mandy the shivers just to look at it. The doorway was still wide open like a gaping mouth, and rocks thrown by the attacker littered the trampled-down grass in front.

"You're right," said Uncle Ross. "No one has lived here in a *looong* time." He strode over to the dark hole and peered in. "Does anyone have a light?"

Three of the four children whipped out their mini flashlights, but Christianne plunked hers in her father's hand first. He snapped it on and waved it around inside. "It's a mess in here," they heard him say. "Hey, what's this?"

The children peeked around him to see what he was talking about. The light beam picked out the metal bed frame still standing on end against the wall.

Nick gulped. "Uh, oh," he said under his breath. "*Now* we're in trouble."

"Have you kids been fooling around in here?" his father asked, suspicion in his voice. "Nick?"

"Uh, we took a look," Nick said, stepping back and trying to remember the story they had agreed on. "A big owl flew out the door and we were curious to see where it came from." He looked at Mandy with pleading eyes. *Help*, he seemed to be saying.

"Uncle Ross, that's where we found the last clue to the puzzle geocache," Mandy said, "behind that wooden owl up on the wall." She had copied the poem from Black Bart's book and now slid the paper out of her pocket and read it aloud.

> *"Ten strides is all from door to tree*
> *Beside the kitchen midden*
> *Remove the rock and strike with spade*
> *To find what has been hidden"*

"That's why we think the stash is nearby," Mandy said. "Ten strides from the door. We figured out a kitchen midden is a dump, so there might be some old junk sticking out of the ground."

Nick jumped in. "We just have to find the right tree and the right rock!"

"Okay," said Uncle Ross. "We'll talk later about going into a dangerous place like this and climbing up on such a risky ladder." He shook his head and added in a mutter, "Kids." He walked back to the doorway. "So, the stride of an average man would be about this long." Starting from the doorway, he took a big step. "We'll have to experiment and see if ten strides will bring us to a tree of any size." He took nine more steps and then looked around. "I don't see anything unusual," he said. "Nick, you try ten strides to the right and I'll do ten to the left." He walked back to the doorway to start again.

Leaping to make his stride equal to his dad's, Nick headed toward the thick woods beside the cabin. His last jump landed him right in a bush. "Ouch!" he said, as its prickly branches raked against his hands. "Darn it!"

"Look, Nick," said Noah, who had been following him. He pointed at a large oak tree arching overhead. "That could be the tree in the poem! It must be pretty old."

Nick rubbed the red scratches on his hands. "Yeah, well, there are plenty of big trees around here." He struggled to remove himself from the bush. "Ooch, ow. . . whoa!" He tripped over something and landed on the ground. . .hard. Nick moaned and sat up. "Who put that rock in the way?"

"Rock?" said Mandy from across the clearing. She had been making ten strides in another direction.

Everyone headed over to where Nick still sat on the ground.

"A tree? A rock?" Christianne said in an excited voice. "Nick, are you sitting on the dump?"

"I dunno," he mumbled. "I don't see anything that looks like trash." He kicked at the decaying leaves with his foot. The rim of an old enamel wash basin stuck up out of the dirt. "On second thought. . ."

"This must be it!" Mandy said. "The cabin's 'kitchen midden.' 'Remove the rock and strike with spade,'" she read from the paper.

"Does that mean to hit the rock with the shovel?" Christianne asked, puzzled.

"No," her mother replied. "I think it means to dig!"

"Come on, Nick," said his father, "help me move the rock."

Nick got up on his knees and together they pushed over the moss-covered stone.

"Eeuw," said Christianne, as bugs crawled into the grass to escape the light.

"No one has uncovered this stash in a long time," said Uncle Ross, "or we've got the wrong spot. Hand me the shovel."

Noah fetched the shovel from beside the front door and trotted over to Uncle Ross with it.

Uncle Ross stuck it in the ground. He was about to jump on it to push it in farther, when a loud growl stunned everyone into silence.

"What's that?" whispered Aunt Ariel. "A b-bear?" She took a step back and gathered the younger children into her arms to protect them.

Another growl issued from the thick bushes. Then the stinkiest smell ever – a combination of rotten eggs, sweaty feet and dirty diapers – drifted to where they stood in a huddle.

"Eeuuw," said Christianne, holding her nose. "It's Bigfoot again!"

"Bigfoot?" Uncle Ross said. "There's no such thing. It's just a myth."

Aunt Ariel pulled the children closer. "Are you sure, Ross?"

"*I'm* sure," said Nick. After all, they had found the costume in the cabin. It didn't mean Bigfoot didn't exist at all, but it meant whoever was trying to chase them away from the stash was an imposter. He grabbed the shovel from his father's hands and lunged at the bushes where the growling came from. "Get out of here, you big hairy monkey!" he yelled. He beat at the bushes with the shovel.

His mother screamed. "Nick! Be careful!"

But instead of attacking, the threatening beast retreated with a yelp and the crackle of breaking branches.

Breathing hard, Nick set down the shovel. "That will sh-show him," he stammered.

The other children gathered around him, patting him on the back.

"Good work, Nick!" said Noah. "You scared him away."

Aunt Ariel held a hand over her heart. "Who was it?"

Mandy shrugged. "We don't know who it is, but *someone's* been pretending to be Bigfoot. He must think we're close to the stash. Let's finish digging."

Uncle Ross took the shovel from Nick and thrust it into the earth. A dull thunk indicated it had hit something. More carefully, Uncle Ross dug down into the dirt.

"There's something here!" he said. He knelt down and cleared soil from around a cylinder shape.

"Hey, it's just like the shapes in the old prospector's drawing!" said Christianne.

"But it's not a battery," Noah said.

Uncle Ross lifted it out of the ground and dusted it off. "It's a can of some kind. . . with a lid." He tried to loosen the top but it was rusted on.

"Here, try this," said Noah, offering the Bigfoot bottle opener he had bought for his father.

Uncle Ross worked it around the rim of the lid. All of a sudden, it popped off. "Oh, my goodness," he said, peering into the can. "I think you kids have found something all right." He smoothed an area on top of the dirt and dumped out the contents. Ten big golden disks clinked onto the ground.

"Are they real, Dad?" Nick asked. He picked one up and rubbed it between his fingers. On one side was a woman's face and on the back was a fancy eagle. Nick squinted at the number below the face. "1856?" he said in wonder.

"Oh, yeah," said his father. They sure *look* real."

"Yahoo!" yelled Christianne. "Treasure!"

"Uncle Ross, we should keep digging – there might be more," said Mandy. She was thinking of the four cylinder shapes on the drawing. So it *was* a treasure map, after all!

"Let's find out," her uncle replied. "Everyone get down around the hole and dig with your hands. We don't want to smash anything with the shovel." First he scooped the gold coins back into the can.

They formed a circle and stuck their fingers in the dirt, feeling around.

"I found one!" Noah shouted and pulled another can from the ground.

"Me too!" squealed Christianne.

Nick and Mandy both grabbed a fourth can at the same time and lifted it out of the hole together.

Uncle Ross levered off the lids with the bottle opener. Each one contained gold coins.

"I think that's all there is," said Mandy. She decided it was time to show Uncle Ross and Aunt Ariel the drawing from the hollow tree. "We found this map, too," she said, pulling it out of her pocket. "It was another clue."

They explored the dirt a little longer, just in case, and then gave up.

"Four it is," said Uncle Ross.

"Gosh," said Aunt Ariel, "there could be a fortune here!"

Chapter 21. The Truth Revealed

"Congratulations, kids, on finding Black Bart's stash," said Blake, standing on the front porch of the camp store. "I've never seen so many gold coins at once."

"Thanks, Blake," Nick replied. "Too bad we can't keep it. Dad said the gold goes to the owners of the campground, since the land we found the treasure on belongs to them." His shoulders slumped in disappointment.

"Actually I should thank *you*," Blake said a little sheepishly. "The owners are my aunt and uncle. They gave me a job here in the summer to help earn some money for college. I had a feeling Black Bart's stash was somewhere near the cabin, but I didn't have time to look for it. I figured the clues would point you in the right direction."

"*You* put the poem in the geocache?" Mandy asked.

"Yeah, that was me," the young man replied. "I knew you were headed there the next day. Mandy, I figured you would choose the peace sign key chain to go with your collection, so I slipped the poem in with it."

"You wrote *all* the poems?" Noah asked, with a puzzled frown.

Blake nodded. "All except the last one. We can assume that Black Bart himself wrote that. I had no idea his book was hidden in the cabin. You kids are good detectives."

Christianne squinted at him. "It's not really fair that we found the treasure and don't get to keep it. Are your aunt and uncle giving *you* some of the gold?"

Blake cleared his throat. "Uh, yeah, in a way. They said they would pay for my college education. That's a huge relief. When I leave college I won't be in debt up to my ears like all my friends."

Christianne crossed her arms. "It's still not fair."

"I agree," said Blake.

"You do?" Christianne asked in surprise.

"Yup." I have something for you from my aunt and uncle. Close your eyes, all of you, and hold out a hand."

The children did as he said.

Blake set a little white box on each person's palm. "Okay, you can open your eyes. . . and open your box."

As each lid was lifted, a gasp sounded.

"Yay!" said Christianne. "We got some treasure!" She lifted the big gold coin out of the box.

"Any gold is good gold!" said Noah.

"You're not kidding," agreed Blake. "The value of gold right now is around $1200 an ounce. These are Double Eagles that were worth $20 when they were minted. Since they weigh almost an ounce each, you can figure out what they're worth now."

"Maybe $1100?" asked Nick, holding his coin up to the light.

"We're rich!" shouted Christianne.

Blake grinned and winked at her. "It's better than a little gold dust in a pan!"

Mandy had been thinking. "So, Blake, if you wanted us to find the stash, who was trying to scare us away?"

"Ah-hem," said Blake. "Somebody here has something to say to you. Mogee?"

Blake's friend, Mogee, sat hunched over in one of the rocking chairs, staring at his feet. A white bandage was wrapped around one of his hands. "Hmm, sorry for scaring you kids," he mumbled.

Nick and Mandy exchanged glances.

"What do you mean?" asked Mandy.

"Come on, Mogee," said Blake. "Tell them. The growls, the footprints, the rocks."

"What?" Nick said. "*You* were Bigfoot?"

"The costume in the cabin!" exclaimed Mandy. "Was that yours?"

"Uh, look," said Mogee. He raised his head and rubbed his good hand against his chin. "You've got to understand. Me and my Pop have been looking for that stash all our lives. We knew it was somewhere nearby. The story got passed down from Great-great Grandpa Bentley."

"That was the old prospector who lived in the hollow tree," explained Blake. "Keep going, Mogee."

Mogee stared out toward the woods. "He knew Black Bart was hiding out in the cabin. He recognized him from a Wanted poster. He figured Bart's stash must be nearby and if he kept an eye on him, eventually he'd lead him to it. Unfortunately, Bart died first. Grandpa Bentley did find a key in the cabin, but he didn't know what it went to. He also found a map but I guess he couldn't make any sense of it. My Pop knew about the key and the map, but he couldn't find either of them. He figured Grandpa hid them somewhere for safe keeping."

"But why did you pretend to be Bigfoot?" Christianne demanded. "That wasn't nice."

For a moment, a spark of anger flashed in Mogee's eyes. "You kids were nosing around. We were afraid you were going to find the stash before we did. So I tried to scare you off."

Mandy frowned at him. "But we heard growls and I saw a face in the window the first night we were here. We hadn't even started exploring then."

Mogee looked away. "Well, it started out as just a joke. When I heard Blake feeding you the Bigfoot legends, it was too good a chance to pass up."

"Are you the one who trapped us in the cabin?" Nick asked. "That could have been dangerous."

Mogee shook his head. "Nah. The message on the wall was from me. But when Pop saw you go in the cabin, he decided to teach you a lesson for snooping. He hammered the door shut. The place is such a shambles, he figured it wouldn't hold you for long, but that a brush with danger would keep you away."

"He doesn't know us," said Mandy, hands on hips. "That just made us more determined to find out what was going on."

"Whatever," Mogee mumbled. "Anyway, it's a done deal now." He stood and ambled toward the porch steps. "Enjoy your gold."

"Wait!" said Noah, holding up his hands to stop him. "One more question. "How did you make the awful smell?"

Mogee snickered. "Home-made stink bombs – they're a blast to make. Put a pin hole in an egg and let it sit for a couple of days. Pew-ee! Then there's the kind where you mix onion, garlic and some burnt hair. That's a good one."

Nick jumped in. "Did you steal the gold-panning equipment?"

Blake raised an eyebrow. "What's this?"

"Hey, man," Mogee said to his friend, "you know I would have brung back your stuff. It was just a joke."

By then, all of them were scowling at the scruffy teen.

He raised his hands, as if in surrender. "Stay cool. I'm leaving now." He backed away from them a few steps and then turned and shuffled down the porch stairs.

"I can't believe that guy!" Nick exclaimed. "He just gets away with all this?"

Blake shrugged. "Well, what he did was kind of mean, but he didn't actually commit a crime. Shoot, all this time, I thought there really was a Bigfoot around. It's kind of disappointing that there isn't." He shrugged again. "Oh, well, all's well that ends well. . . So, would you kids like to borrow the gold-panning equipment and try again?"

Mandy and Nick looked at each other and shook their heads.

"Naw," said Nick. "We've got a gold coin each, so I think we're all set."

"Tomorrow's our last day here," added Mandy. "Uncle Ross and Aunt Ariel are taking us on another geocache hunt, a Level 2 search."

"It's more fun when you know you'll actually find something," said Christianne.

"Even if it's just a Bigfoot bottle opener!" agreed Noah, pulling his out of his pocket.

Everyone laughed.

That evening the four children sat around the campfire toasting marshmallows.

"Hey, Noah," said Nick, "I have something for you." He handed the boy a Bigfoot bottle opener. "I thought you might like to have one of your own, since you're giving the other one to your dad. It sure came in handy."

"Thanks, Nick," said Noah. "It will remind me of our fun adventure here." He stowed it in his camper shorts.

Mandy turned her stick to brown her marshmallow evenly. "Well, Nick, I have to say you almost had me convinced that Bigfoot is real. It just goes to show you that people will do all kinds of things to keep a hoax going."

"What's a hoax?" asked Christianne.

"It's tricking someone into believing something crazy," Mandy answered.

"I don't know," Nick said. "That Mogee put on a pretty convincing act. But that doesn't mean Bigfoot isn't real." Nick's marshmallow burst into flames and turned black. "Crud," he said. "Now I have to start over. I hate them burnt!" He flung the charred lump into the bushes.

Something rustled in the same spot in the undergrowth and growled.

The four children stared at each other.

"Mogee?" whispered Noah.

"He wouldn't dare do it again," Mandy said. "Would he?"

Another growl came from the bushes. Then the nostril-twitching odor of rotten eggs floated through the clearing.

"Oh, no," said Christianne. "Look!" She pointed at two reddish eyes gleaming between the branches.

"It's Bigfoot – for real!" shouted Nick. "R-r-run!"

The kids tossed their sticks, marshmallows and all, into the fire and raced to the cabin.

A tall hairy creature loped out of the woods, grabbed the bag of marshmallows in one huge hand, and melted into the darkness.

Author's Note

Readers always wonder where a writer comes up with his or her ideas for a story. The following is my inspiration for writing *The Outlaw's Key*.

In the summer of 2012 I traveled to northern California and visited the Armstrong Redwoods Natural Preserve and the Navarro River Redwoods State Park. The ancient, towering sequoias in the mist-shrouded forests conjured up thoughts of Sasquatch legends. Whether Bigfoot really exists, I do not know, but standing beneath those primeval giants you feel like anything is possible. I crawled into the hollow trunk of one of the redwoods which sparked my imagination. Certainly Bigfoot – or a person -- could live in such a place!

When I was about Mandy's age, my brothers and I planned to spend the night in a deserted cabin in the woods not far from our home in Maine. As we settled into our blankets, we heard scratching on the outside wall. It would have been smart to stay where we were, but scared as we were, we hightailed it for home. The next day when we went back to get our stuff, we found furrows raked down through the tar paper covering one of the outside walls. We figured it was a bear trying to get to the food we had brought along as a bed time snack!

The outlaws mentioned in the story were real people. Charles E. Bowles, alias Black Bart, was regarded as a 'gentleman bandit' and addressed his victims with polite words. In his 28 stagecoach robberies, he never shot anyone and he did leave poems behind at a couple of holdup spots. After spending four years in prison, he swore he was done with a life of crime and wanted to go off and be by himself. After that he pretty much vanished. No one knows exactly where or when he died.

In March of 2014, I read in the newspaper about a northern California couple who found a stash of gold on their property while out walking their dog. They found eight decaying metal cans containing 1400 gold coins, now worth $10 million! It is thought to be the hidden loot of an outlaw, maybe Black Bart himself.

Geocaching, a form of treasure-hunting using GPS, is all the rage now. There are thousands of caches stashed all over the world and millions of avid geocachers searching for them. They range from a one-star easy-to-find cache to a 6-star cache that might be in a very small container hidden in a challenging location. If you are interested in finding out more about it, check out the official website, **www.geocaching.com**.

Like the other Key Mysteries, *The Outlaw's Key* is a melding of history, legends, personal experience, facts and fiction. It was lots of fun to write and I hope you enjoyed reading it!

~ Angeli Perrow

BOOKS BY ANGELI PERROW

The Key Mystery Series for 8-12 year olds:

The Lightkeeper's Key
The Whispering Key
The Ghost Miner's Key
The Buccaneer's Key
The Outlaw's Key

The Celtic Series for teens:

Celtic Thunder
Celtic Tide

Picture Books:

Captain's Castaway
Lighthouse Dog to the Rescue
Sirius the Dog Star
Many Hands: A Penobscot Indian Story
          (Lupine Award Winner)
Dogsled Dreamer
Love From the Sky

Learn more at:
www.angeliperrow.com

Made in the USA
Charleston, SC
12 December 2014